The Sleeping Beauty

and other fairy tales

And there, on a bed the curtains of which were drawn wide, he beheld the loveliest vision he had ever seen.

The Sleeping Beauty

and other fairy tales

FROM THE OLD FRENCH

retold by

Sir Arthur Quiller-Couch

illustrated by

Edmund Dulac

WEATHERVANE BOOKS
NEW YORK

This edition was originally published by Hodder and Stoughton.

This edition is published by Weathervane Books,
distributed by Crown Publishers, Inc.

a b c d e f g h

WEATHERVANE 1978 PRINTING
Manufactured in the United States of America

Library of Congress Cataloging in Publication Data
Quiller-Couch, Arthur Thomas, Sir, 1863-1944.
The sleeping beauty and other fairy tales from the old French.
Reprint of the 1910 ed. published by Hodder and Stoughton, New York.
CONTENTS: The sleeping beauty.—Blue Beard.—Cinderella. [etc.]
1. Fairy tales, French. [1. Fairy tales. 2. Folklore—France] I. Dulac, Edmund. II. Title.
PZ8.Q42Sl 1978 [398.2] 78-12931
ISBN 0-517-26292-4

PREFACE

ONCE upon a time I found myself halting between two projects, both magnificent. For the first, indeed—which was to discover, digest and edit all the fairy tales in the world—I was equipped neither with learning, nor with command of languages, nor with leisure, nor with length of years. It is a task for many men, clubbing their lifetimes together. But the second would have cost me quite a respectable amount of toil ; for it was to translate and annotate the whole collection of stories in the *Cabinet des Fées*.

Preface

Now the *Cabinet des Fées*, in the copy on my shelves, extends to forty-one volumes, printed, as their title-pages tell, at Geneva between the years 1785 and 1789, and published in Paris by M. Cuchet, Rue et Hôtel Serpente. The dates may set us moralising. While the Rue Serpente unfolded, as though

Tranquilla per alta,

its playful voluminous coils, the throne of France with the Ancien Régime rocked closer and closer to catastrophe. In 1789 (July), just as M. Cuchet (good man and leisurable to the end) wound up his series with a last volume of the *Suite des Mille et Un Nuits*, they toppled over with the fall of the Bastille.

Even so in England—we may remind ourselves—in 1653, when the gods made Oliver Cromwell Protector, Izaak Walton chose to publish a book about little fishes. But the reminder is not quite apposite : for angling, the contemplative man's recreation, was no favourite or characteristic or symbolical pursuit of the Order which Cromwell overthrew (and, besides, he did not overthrow it) ;

whereas, M. Cuchet's forty-one volumes most pertinently as well as amply illustrated some real qualities, and those the most amiable of the Ancien Régime. When we think of the French upper classes from the days of Louis XIV. to the Revolution, we associate them with a certain elegance, a taste fastidious and polite, if artificial, in the arts of living and the furniture of life; and in this we do them justice. But, if I mistake not, we seldom credit them with the quality which more than any other struck the contemporary foreign observer who visited France with a candid mind—I mean their good temper. We allow the Bastille or the guillotine to cast their shadows backward over this period, or we see it distorted in the glare of Burke's rhetoric or of Carlyle's lurid and fuliginous history. But if we go to an eyewitness, Arthur Young, who simply reported what he saw, having no rhetorical axe to grind or guillotine to sharpen, we get a totally different impression. The last of Young's *Travels in France* (1787-1789) actually coincided with the close of M. Cuchet's pleasant enterprise in publishing; and I do not think it fanciful to suppose that, had this very practical

Englishman found time to read at large in the *Cabinet des Fées*, he would have discovered therein much to corroborate the evidence steadily and unconsciously borne by his own journals—that the urbanity of life among the French upper classes was genuine, reflecting a real and (for a whole society) a remarkable sunniness of disposition. Unconscious of their doom, the little victims played. But they did play; and they fell victims, not to their own passions, but to a form of government economically rotten.

Of all the volumes in the *Cabinet*, possibly the most famous are the first and second, containing the fairy tales of Charles Perrault and Madame d'Aulnoy, and vols. 7-11, containing M. Galland's version (so much better than any translation) of *The Arabian Nights*. I hope that one of those days Mr. Dulac will lay the public under debt by illustrating all these, and the stories of Antony Hamilton to boot. Meanwhile, here are three of the most famous tales from Perrault's wallet, and one, the evergreen *Beauty and the Beast*, by an almost forgotten authoress, Madame de Villeneuve.

The ghost of Charles Perrault, could it walk

to-day—*perruque* and all—might well sigh over the vanity of human pretensions. For Monsieur Perrault was a person of importance in his lifetime (1628-1703), and a big-wig in every sense of the term. Colbert made him Secretary of the Academy of Inscriptions, and anon Controller of Public Works—in which capacity he suggested to his architect-brother, Claude Perrault, the façade of the Louvre with its renowned colonnade. He flattered his monarch with a poem *Le Siècle de Louis le Grand.* 'Je ne sais,' observes a circle, 'si ce roi, malgré son amour excessif pour la flatterie, fut content : les bornes étaient outrepassées.' The poem, as a poem, had little success; but by positing that the Age of Louis was the greatest in history, and suggesting that the moderns were as good as the ancients or better, it started a famous controversy. Boileau, Racine, La Bruyère, honoured him by taking the other side, and forced him to develop his paradox in a book of dialogues, *Parallèles des Anciens et des Modernes.* But his best answer was his urbane remark (for he kept his temper admirably) that these gentlemen did ill to dispute the superiority of the moderns while their own works gave proof of it. He wrote other poems, other tractates (including one on the 'Illustrious Men of his Age'), besides occasional tracts on matters of high politics: and his memory is kept alive by one small packet of fairy-tales—stories which he heard the nurse telling his little boy, and set down upon paper for a recreation! That is the way with literary fame. To take an English example: it is odds that Southey, poet-laureate and politician of great self-importance in his day, will come finally to be remembered by his baby-story of *The Three Bears*. It will certainly outlive *Thalaba the Destroyer*, and possibly even the *Life of Nelson*.

As for Gabrielle Susanne, wife of M. de Gallon, Seigneur de Villeneuve and lieutenant-colonel of infantry (whom she outlived), she wrote a number of romantic stories—*Le Phénix Conjugal*, *Le Juge Parvenu*, *Le Beau-Frère Supposé*, *La Jardinière de Vincennes*, *Le Prince Azerolles*, etc. I am not—perhaps few are—acquainted with these works. Madame de Villeneuve died in 1755 and lives only by grace of her *La Belle et La Bête*; and that again lives in despite of its literary defects. It has style ; but the style inheres neither in its language, which is loose, nor in its construction. The story, as she wrote it, tails off woefully and drags to an end in mere foolishness.

Since Perrault, who is usually accepted as the fountainhead of these charming French fairy-stories, belongs almost entirely to the seventeenth century, it may be asked why Mr. Dulac has chosen to depict his Princes and Princess in costumes of the eighteenth? Well, for my part, I hold that he has obeyed a just instinct in choosing the period when the literature he illustrates was at the acme of its vogue. But his designs, in every stroke of which the style of that period is so unerringly felt, provide his best apology.

My own share in this volume is, perhaps, less easily defended. I began by translating Perrault's tales, very nearly word for word; because to me his style has always seemed nearly perfect for its purpose; and the essence of 'style' in writing is propriety to its purpose. On the other hand the late M. Ferdinand Brunetière has said that Perrault's is 'devoid of charm,' and on this subject M. Brunetière's opinion must needs out-value mine ten times over. Certainly the translations, when finished, did not satisfy me, and so I turned back to the beginning and have rewritten the stories in my own way, which (as you may say with the Irish butler) 'may not be the best claret, but 'tis the best ye 've got.'

I have made bold, too, to omit Perrault's conclusion of *La Belle au Bois Dormant*. To my amazement the editor of the *Cabinet des Fées* selects this lame sequel—it is no better than a sequel—of a lovely tale, and assigns to it the credit of having established 'la véritable fortune de ce genre.' Frankly, I cannot believe him. Further, I have condensed Madame de Villeneuve's narrative and obliterated its feeble ending. In taking each of these liberties I have the warrant of tradition, which in the treatment of fairy-tales speaks with a voice more authoritative than the original author's, for it speaks with the united voices of many thousands of children, his audience and best critics. As the children have decreed that in Southey's tale of *The Three Bears* the heroine shall be a little girl, and not, as Southey invented her, a good-for-nothing old woman, so they have decreed the story of *The Sleeping Beauty* to end with the Prince's kiss, and that of *Beauty and the Beast* with the Beast's transformation. And as *Beauty and the Beast* is really but a variant of the immortal fable of *Cupid and Psyche*, I might — had I room to spare — attempt to prove to you that the children's taste is here, as usually, right and classical.

ARTHUR QUILLER-COUCH

ILLUSTRATIONS

THE SLEEPING BEAUTY

Illustrations

Illustrations

Illustrations

THE SLEEPING BEAUTY

ONCE upon a time there lived a King and a Queen, who lacked but one thing on earth to make them entirely happy. The *King* was young, handsome, and wealthy ; the *Queen* had a nature as good and gentle as her face was beautiful ; and they adored one another, having married for love—which among kings and queens is not always the rule. Moreover, they reigned over a kingdom at peace, and their people were devoted to them. What more, then, could they possibly want ?

Well, they wanted one thing very badly, and the lack of it grieved them more than words can tell. They had no child. Vows, pilgrimages, all ways were tried; yet for a long while nothing came of it all, and the poor *Queen* especially was in despair.

At last, however, to her own and her husband's inexpressible joy, she gave birth to a daughter. As soon as the palace guns announced this event, the whole nation went wild with delight. Flags waved everywhere, bells were set pealing until the steeples rocked, crowds tossed up their hats and cheered, while the soldiers presented arms, and even strangers meeting in the street fell upon each other's neck, exclaiming: 'Our *Queen* has a daughter! Yes, yes—Our *Queen* has a daughter! Long live the little *Princess*!'

A name had now to be found for the royal babe; and the *King* and *Queen*, after talking over some scores of names, at length decided to call her *Aurora*, which means *The Dawn*. The Dawn itself (thought they) was never more beautiful than this darling of theirs. The next business, of course, was to hold a christening. They agreed that it must be a magnificent one; and as a first step they invited all the Fairies they could find in the land to be godmothers to the *Princess Aurora*; that each one of them might bring her a gift, as was the custom with Fairies in those days, and so she might have all the perfections imaginable. After making long inquiries—for I should tell you that all this happened not so many hundred years ago, when Fairies were already growing somewhat scarce—they found seven. But this again pleased them, because seven is a lucky number.

After the ceremonies of the christening, while the trumpeters sounded their fanfares and the guns boomed out again from the great tower, all the company returned to the Royal Palace to find a great feast arrayed. Seats of honour had been set for the seven fairy godmothers, and before each was laid a dish of honour, with a dish-cover of solid gold, and beside the dish a spoon, a knife, and a fork, all of pure gold and all set with diamonds and rubies. But just as they were seating themselves at table, to the dismay of every one there appeared in the doorway an old crone, dressed in black and leaning on a crutched stick. Her chin and her hooked nose almost met together, like a pair of nut-crackers, for she had very few teeth remaining ; but between them she growled to the guests in a terrible voice :

'I am the Fairy *Uglyane*! Pray where are your King's manners, that I have not been invited?'

She had in fact been overlooked; and this was not surprising, because she lived at the far end of the country, in a lonely tower set around by the forest. For fifty years she had never come out of this tower, and every one believed her to be dead or enchanted. That, you must know, is the commonest way the Fairies have of ending: they lock themselves up in a tower or within a hollow oak, and are never seen again.

The *King*, though she chose to accuse his manners, was in fact the politest of men. He hurried to express his regrets, led her to table with his own hand, and ordered a dish to be set for her; but with the best will in the world he could not give her a dish-cover such as the others had, because seven only had been made for the seven invited Fairies. The old crone received his excuses very ungraciously, while accepting a seat. It was plain that she had taken deep offence. One of the younger Fairies, *Hippolyta* by name, who sat by, overheard her mumbling threats between her teeth; and fearing she might bestow some unlucky gift upon the little *Princess*, went as soon as she rose from table and hid herself close by the cradle, behind the tapestry, that she might have the last word and undo, so far as she could, what evil the Fairy *Uglyane* might have in her mind.

She had scarcely concealed herself before the other Fairies began to advance, one by one, to bestow their gifts on the *Princess*. The youngest promised her that she should be the most beautiful creature in the world ; the next, that she should have the wit of an angel; the third, a marvellous grace in all her ways ; the fourth, that she should dance to perfection ; the fifth, that she should sing like a nightingale ; the sixth, that she should play exquisitely on all instruments of music.

Now came the turn of the old Fairy *Uglyane*. Her head nodded with spite and old age together, as she bent over the cradle and shook her crutched staff above the head of the pretty babe, who slept on sweetly, too young and too innocent as yet to dream of any such thing as mischief in this world.

'This is my gift to you, *Princess Aurora*,' announced the hag, still in her creaking voice that shook as spitefully as her body. 'I promise that one day you shall pierce your hand with a spindle, and on that day you shall surely die!'

At these terrible words the poor *Queen* fell back fainting into her husband's arms. A trembling seized the whole Court; the ladies were in tears, and the younger lords and knights were calling out to seize and burn the wicked witch, when the young Fairy stepped forth from behind the tapestry, and passing by *Uglyane*, who stood scornful in the midst of this outcry, she thus addressed their Majesties:—

'Take comfort, O *King* and *Queen*: your daughter shall not die thus. It is true, I have not the power wholly to undo what this elder sister of mine has done. The *Princess* must indeed pierce her hand with a spindle; but, instead of dying, she shall only fall into a deep slumber that shall last for many, many years, at the end of which a King's son shall come and awake her. Whenever this misfortune happens to your little *Aurora*, do not doubt that I, the Fairy *Hippolyta*, her godmother, shall get news of it and come at once to render what help I may.'

The *King*, while declaring himself infinitely obliged to the good Fairy *Hippolyta*, could not help feeling that hers was but cold comfort at the best. He gave orders to close the christening festivities at once, although the Fairy *Uglyane*, their spoil-joy, had already taken her departure; passing unharmed through the crowd of folk, every one of whom wished her ill, and riding away—it was generally agreed—upon a broomstick.

To satisfy the *King's* faithful subjects, however,—who were unaware of any misadventure—the palace fireworks were duly let off, with a grand set-piece wishing *Long Life to the Princess Aurora!* in all the colours of the rainbow. But His Majesty, after bowing from the balcony amid the banging of rockets and hissing of Catherine wheels, retired to a private room with his Chamberlain, and there, still amid the noise of explosions and cheering, drew up the first harsh proclamation of his reign. It forbade every one, on pain of death, to use a spindle in spinning or even to have a spindle in his house. Heralds took copies of this proclamation and marched through the land reading it, to the sound of trumpets, from every market-place: and it gravely puzzled and distressed all who listened, for their women folk prided themselves on their linen. Its fineness was a byword throughout the neighbouring kingdoms, and they knew themselves to be famous for it. ‘But what sort of linen,’ said they, ‘would His Majesty have us spin without spindles?’

They had a great affection, however (as we have seen), for their monarch; and for fifteen or sixteen years all the spinning-wheels were silent throughout the land. The little *Princess Aurora* grew up without ever having seen one. But one day—the *King* and *Queen* being absent at one of their country houses—she gave her governess the slip, and running at will through the palace and upstairs from one chamber to another, she came at length to a turret with a winding staircase, from the top of which a strange whirring sound attracted her and seemed to invite her to climb. As she mounted after the sound, on a sudden it ceased; but still she followed the stairs and came, at the very top, to an open door through which she looked in upon a small garret where sat an honest old woman alone, winding her distaff. The good soul had never, in sixteen years, heard of the *King's* prohibition against spindles;

and this is just the sort of thing that happens in palaces.

'What are you doing, goody?' asked the *Princess.*

'I am spinning, pretty one,' answered the old woman, who did not know who she was.

'Spinning? What is that?'

'I wonder sometimes,' said the old woman, 'what the world is coming to, in these days!' And that, of course, was natural enough, and might occur to anybody after living so long as she had lived in a garret on the top of a tower. 'Spinning,' she said wisely, 'is spinning, or was; and, gentle or simple, no one is fit to keep house until she has learnt to spin.'

'But how pretty it is!' said the *Princess.* 'How do you do it? Give it to me and let me see if I can do so well.'

She had no sooner grasped the spindle—she was over-eager perhaps, or just a little bit clumsy, or maybe the fairy decree had so ordained it—than it pierced her hand and she dropped down in a swoon.

The old trot in a flurry ran to the head of the

stairs and called for help. There was no bell rope, and, her voice being weak with age and her turret in the remotest corner of the palace, it was long before any one heard her in the servants' hall. The servants, too—in the absence of the *King* and *Queen*—were playing cards, and could not be interrupted by anybody until their game was finished. Then they sat down and discussed whose business it was to attend on a call from that particular turret; and this again proved to be a nice point, since nobody could remember having been summoned thither, and all were against setting up a precedent (as they called it). In the end they decided to send up the lowest of the junior page-boys. But he had a weakness which he somehow forgot to mention—that of fainting at the sight of blood. So when he reached the garret and fainted, the old woman had to begin screaming over again.

This time they sent up a scullery maid; who, being good-natured and unused to the ways of the palace, made the best haste she could to the garret, whence presently she returned with the terrible news. The servants, who had gone back to their game, now dropped their cards and came running.

All the household, in fact, came pouring up the turret stairs; the palace physicians themselves crowding in such numbers that the poor *Princess Aurora* would have been hard put to it for fresh air could fresh air have restored her. They dashed water on her face, unlaced her, slapped her hands, tickled the soles of her feet, burned feathers under her nose, rubbed her temples with Hungary-water. They held consultations over her, by twos and threes, and again in Grand Committee. But nothing would bring her to.

Meanwhile, a messenger had ridden off post-haste with the tidings, and while the doctors were still consulting and shaking their heads the *King* himself came galloping home to the palace. In the midst of his grief he bethought him of what the Fairies had foretold; and being persuaded that, since they had said it, this was fated to happen, he blamed no one but gave orders to carry the *Princess* to the finest apartment in the palace, and there lay her on a bed embroidered with gold and silver.

At sight of her, she was so lovely, you might well have supposed that some bright being of the skies had floated down to earth and there dropped asleep after her long journey. For her swoon had not taken away the warm tints of her complexion : her cheeks were like carnations, her lips like coral : and though her eyes were closed and the long lashes would not lift, her soft breathing told that she was not dead. The *King* commanded them all to leave her and let her sleep in peace until the hour of her awakening should arrive.

Now when the accident befell our *Princess* the good Fairy *Hippolyta*, who had saved her life, happened to be in the Kingdom of Mataquin, twelve thousand leagues away ; but news of it was brought to her in an incredibly short space of time by a little dwarf who owned a pair of seven-league boots. (These were boots in which you could walk seven leagues at a single stride.) She set off at once to the help of her beloved god-daughter, and behold in an hour this good Fairy arrived at the palace, in a fiery chariot drawn by dragons.

Our *King* met her and handed her down from the chariot. She approved of all that he had done; but, greatly foreseeing as she was, she bethought her that, as all mortals perish within a hundred years or so, when the time came for the *Princess* to awake she would be distressed at finding herself orphaned and alone in this old castle.

So this is what she did. She touched with her wand everything and everybody in the palace : the *King*, the *Queen* ; the ministers and privy councillors ; the archbishop (who was the Grand Almoner), the bishops and the minor clergy ; the maids-of-honour, ladies of the bedchamber, governesses, gentlemen-in-waiting, equerries, heralds, physicians, officers, masters of the household, cooks, scullions, lackeys, guards, Switzers, pages, footmen. She touched the *Princess's* tutors and the Court professors in the midst of their deep studies. She touched likewise all the horses in the stables, with the grooms; the huge mastiffs in the yard; even *Tiny*, the *Princess's* little pet dog, and *Fluff*, her black-and-white cat, that lay coiled on a cushion by her bedside.

The instant the Fairy *Hippolyta* touched them they all fell asleep, not to awake until the same moment as their mistress, that all might be ready to wait on her when she needed them. The very spits at the fire went to sleep, loaded as they were with partridges and pheasants; and the fire went to sleep too. All this was done in a moment: the Fairies were never long about their business in those days.

But it so happened that one of the *King's* councillors, the Minister of Marine (his office dated from a previous reign when the kingdom had hoped to conquer and acquire a seaboard) had overslept himself that morning and came late to the palace without any knowledge of what had befallen. He felt no great fear that his unpunctuality would be remarked, the *King* (as he supposed) being absent in the country; nevertheless he took the precaution of letting himself in by a small postern door, and so missed being observed by the Fairy and touched by her wand. Entering his office, and perceiving that his under-secretary (usually so brisk) and all his clerks rested their heads on their desks in attitudes of sleep, he drew the conclusion that something had happened, for he was an excellent judge of natural slumber. The farther he penetrated into the palace, the stronger his suspicions became. He withdrew on tiptoe. Though by nature and habit a lazy man, he was capable of sudden decision, and returning to his home he caused notices to be posted up, forbidding any one to approach the castle, the inmates of which were suffering from an Eastern but temporary affliction known as the Sleeping Sickness.

These notices were unnecessary, for within a few hours there grew up, all around the park, such a number of trees of all sizes, and such a tangle of briars and undergrowth, that neither beast nor man could find a passage. They grew until nothing but the tops of the castle towers could be seen, and these only from a good way off. There was no mistake about it : the Fairy had done her work well, and the *Princess* might sleep with no fear of visits from the inquisitive.

One day, many, many years afterwards, the incomparable young *Prince Florimond* happened to ride a-hunting on that side of the country which lay next to the tangled forest, and asked : 'What were those towers he saw pushing up above the midst of a great thick wood ?'

They all answered him as they heard tell. Some said it was an old castle haunted by ghosts.

All the company returned to the Royal Palace to find a great feast arrayed.

Her head nodded with spite and old age together,
as she bent over the cradle.

'I am spinning, pretty one,' answered the old woman, who did not know who she was.

But news of it was brought to her by a little dwarf, who owned a pair of seven-league boots.

She touched the Princess's tutors and the Court professors in the midst of their deep studies.

They grew until nothing but the tops of the castle towers could be seen.

The ruddy faces of the switzers ..
told him that they were no worse than asleep.

Others, that all the wizards and witches of the country met there to keep Sabbath.

The most general opinion was that an Ogre dwelt there, and that he carried off thither all the children he could catch, to eat them at his ease. No one could follow him, for he alone knew how to find a passage through the briars and brambles. The *Prince* could not tell which to believe of all these informants, for all gave their versions with equal confidence, as commonly happens with those who talk on matters of which they can know nothing for certain. He was turning from one to another in perplexity, when a peasant spoke up and said :—

'Your Highness, long ago I heard my father tell that there was in yonder castle a Princess, the most beautiful that ever man saw; that she must lie asleep there for many, many years; and that one day she will be awakened by a King's son, for whom she was destined.'

At these words *Prince Florimond* felt himself a-fire. He believed, without weighing it, that he could accomplish this fine adventure; and, spurred on by love and ambition, he resolved to explore then and there and discover the truth for himself.

Leaping down from his horse he started to run towards the wood, and had almost reached the edge of it before the attendant courtiers guessed his design. They called to him to come back, but he ran on, and was about to fling himself boldly into the undergrowth, when as by magic all the great trees, the shrubs, the creepers, the ivies, briars and brambles, unlaced themselves of their own accord and drew aside to let him pass. He found himself within a long glade or avenue, at the end of which glimmered the walls of an old castle ; and towards this he strode. It surprised him somewhat that none of his attendants were following him ; the reason being that as soon as he had passed through it, the undergrowth drew close as ever again. He heard their voices, fainter and fainter behind him, beyond the barrier, calling, beseeching him to desist. But he held on his way without one backward look. He was a Prince, and young, and therefore valiant.

He came to the castle, and pushing aside the ivies that hung like a curtain over the gateway, entered a wide outer court and stood still for a moment, holding his breath, while his eyes travelled over a scene that might well have frozen them with terror. The court was silent, dreadfully silent; yet it was by no means empty. On all hands lay straight, stiff bodies of men and beasts, seemingly all dead. Nevertheless, as he continued to gaze, his courage returned; for the pimpled noses and ruddy faces of the Switzers told him that they were no worse than asleep; and their cups, which yet held a few heeltaps of wine, proved that they had fallen asleep over a drinking-bout.

He stepped by them and passed across a second great court paved with marble; he mounted a broad flight of marble steps leading to the main doorway; he entered a guardroom, just within the doorway, where the guards stood in rank with shouldered muskets, every man of them asleep and snoring his best. He made his way through a number of rooms filled with ladies and gentlemen, some standing, others sitting, but all asleep. He drew aside a heavy purple curtain, and once more held his breath; for he was looking into the great Hall of State where, at a long table, sat and slumbered the *King* with his Council. The Lord Chancellor slept in the act of dipping pen into inkpot; the Archbishop in the act of taking snuff; and between the spectacles on the Archbishop's nose and the spectacles on the Lord Chancellor's a spider had spun a beautiful web.

Prince Florimond tiptoed very carefully past these august sleepers and, leaving the hall by another door, came to the foot of the grand staircase. Up this, too, he went; wandered along a corridor to his right, and, stopping by hazard at one of the many doors, opened it and looked into a bath-room lined with mirrors and having in its midst, sunk in the floor, a huge round basin of whitest porcelain wherein a spring of water bubbled deliciously. Three steps led down to the bath, and at the head of them stood a couch, with towels, and court-suit laid ready, exquisitely embroidered and complete to the daintiest of lace ruffles and the most delicate of body linen.

Then the *Prince* bethought him that he had ridden far before ever coming to the wood; and the mirrors told him that he was also somewhat travel-stained from his passage through it. So, having by this time learnt to accept any new wonder without question, he undressed himself and took a bath, which he thoroughly enjoyed. Nor was he altogether astonished, when he tried on the clothes, to find that they fitted him perfectly. Even the rosetted shoes of satin might have been made to his measure.

Having arrayed himself thus hardily, he resumed his quest along the corridor. The very next door he tried opened on a chamber all panelled with white and gold ; and there, on a bed the curtains of which were drawn wide, he beheld the loveliest vision he had ever seen : a Princess, seemingly about seventeen or eighteen years old, and of a beauty so brilliant that he could not have believed this world held the like.

But she lay still, so still ! . . . *Prince Florimond* drew near, trembling and wondering, and sank on his knees beside her. Still she lay, scarcely seeming to breathe, and he bent and touched with his lips the little hand that rested, light as a rose-leaf, on the coverlet. . . .

With that, as the long spell of her enchantment came to an end, the *Princess* awaked ; and looking at him with eyes more tender than a first sight of him might seem to excuse :—

'Is it you, my *Prince*?' she said. 'You have been a long while coming!'

The *Prince*, charmed by these words, and still more by the manner in which they were spoken, knew not how to find words for the bliss in his heart. He assured her that he loved her better than his own self. Their speech after this was not very coherent; they gazed at one another for longer stretches than they talked; but if eloquence lacked, there was plenty of love. He, to be sure, showed the more embarrassment; and no need to wonder at this—she had had time to think over what to say to him; for I hold it not unlikely (though the story does not say anything of this) that the good Fairy *Hippolyta* had taken care to amuse her, during her long sleep, with some pleasurable dreams. In short, the *Princess Aurora* and the *Prince Florimond* conversed for four hours, and still without saying the half they had to say.

Meanwhile all the palace had awaked with the *Princess*. In the Council Chamber the *King* opened his eyes and requested the Lord Chancellor to read that last sentence of his over again a little more distinctly. The Lord Chancellor, dipping his quill into the dry inkpot, asked the Archbishop in a whisper how many t's there were in 'regrettable.' The Archbishop, taking a pinch of snuff that had long ago turned to dust, answered with a terrific sneeze, which again was drowned by the striking of all the clocks in the palace, as they started frantically to make up for lost time. Dogs barked, doors banged; the *Princess's* parrot screamed in his cage and was answered by the peacocks squawking from the terrace; amid which hubbub the Minister for Agriculture, forgetting his manners, made a trumpet of his hands and bawled across the table, begging His Majesty to adjourn for dinner. In short, every one's first thought was of his own business; and, as they were not all in love, they were ready to die with hunger.

Even the *Queen*, who had dropped asleep while discussing with her maids-of-honour the shade of mourning which most properly expressed regret for royal personages in a trance, lost her patience at length, and sent one of her attendants with word that she, for her part, was keen-set for something to eat, and that in her young days it had been customary for young ladies released from enchantment to accept the congratulations of their parents without loss of time. The *Prince Florimond*, by this message recalled to his devoirs, helped the *Princess* to rise. She was completely dressed, and very magnificently too.

Taking his beloved *Princess Aurora* by the hand, he led her to her parents, who embraced her passionately and—their first transports over—turned to welcome him as a son, being charmed (quite apart from their gratitude) by the modest gallantry of his address. They passed into a great dining-room lined with mirrors, where they supped and were served by the royal attendants. Violins and hautboys discoursed music that was ancient indeed, but excellent, and the meal was scarcely concluded before the company enjoyed a very pleasant surprise.

Prince Florimond, having no eyes but for his love, might be excused if he forgot that his attendants must, long before now, have carried home their report, and that his parents would be in deep distress, wondering what had become of him. But the *King*, the *Princess's* father, had a truly royal habit of remembering details, especially when it concerned setting folks at their ease. Before dinner he had dispatched a messenger to carry word to *Prince Florimond's* father, that his son was safe, and to acquaint him briefly with what had befallen. The messenger, riding through the undergrowth—which now obligingly parted before him as it had, a while ago, to admit the *Prince*—and arriving at the outskirts of the wood, found there a search-party vainly endeavouring to break through the barrier, with the *Prince's* aged father standing by and exhorting them in person, to whom he delivered his message. Trembling with relief—for he truly supposed his son to be lost beyond recall—the old man entreated the messenger to turn back and escort him. So he arrived, and was ushered into the hall.

The situation, to be sure, was delicate. But when these two kings, both so well meaning, had met and exchanged courtesies, and the one had raised the other by the hand to a place on the daïs beside him, already and without speech they had almost accorded.

'I am an old man,' said the *Prince's* father; 'I

have reigned long enough for my satisfaction, and now care for little in life but to see my son happy.'

'I think I can promise you that,' said the *Princess's* father, smiling, with a glance at the two lovers.

'I am old enough, at any rate, to have done with ambitions,' said the one.

'And I,' said the other, 'have dreamed long enough, at any rate, to despise them. What matters ruling to either of us two, while we see your son and my daughter reigning together?'

So it was agreed, then and there; and after supper, without loss of time, the Archbishop married the *Prince Florimond* and the *Princess Aurora* in the chapel of the Castle. The two Kings and the *Princess's* mother saw them to their chamber, and the first maid-of-honour drew the curtain. They slept little—the *Princess* had no occasion; but the *Prince* next morning led his bride back to the city, where they were acclaimed by the populace and lived happy ever after, reigning in prosperity and honour.

The Sleeping Beauty

MORAL

Ye Maids, to await some while a lover fond,
Rich, titled, debonair as Florimond,
Is reason ; and who learns on fate to attend
Goes seldom unrewarded in the end—
'What ! No one kiss us for a hundred years !'
There, la-la-la ! I understood, my dears.

ANOTHER

Further, the story would suggest a doubt
That marriage may *be happiest when deferr'd—*
'Deferr'd ?' you cry—'Deferr'd,' I see you pout,
—We'll skip this moral, and attempt a third.

ANOTHER

Thirdly, our fable then appears to prove
Disparity of years no bar to love.
Crabb'd Age and Youth—But that's an ancient quarrel,
And I'll not interfere. There's no third moral.

BLUE BEARD

IN the East, in a city not far from Baghdad, there lived a man who had many possessions and might have been envied by all who knew him had these possessions been less by one. He had fine houses in town and country, retinues of servants, gold and silver plate in abundance, coffers heaped with jewels, costly carpets, embroidered furniture, cabinets full of curiosities, gilded coaches, teams of Arab horses of the purest breed. But unluckily he had also a blue beard, which made him so frightfully ugly that every woman wanted to scream and run away at sight of him.

Among his neighbours was a lady of quality,

who had two sons and two daughters. Upon these two damsels *Blue Beard* cast his affections, without knowing precisely which he preferred; and asked the lady to bestow the hand of one of her daughters upon him, adding, not too tactfully, that he would leave the choice to her. Neither *Anne* nor *Fatima* was eager for the honour. They sent their suitor to and fro, and back again from one to the other: they really could not make up their minds to accept a husband with a blue beard. It increased their repugnance (for they were somewhat romantic young ladies) to learn that he had already married several wives; and, moreover, nobody could tell what had become of them, which again was not reassuring.

Blue Beard, to make their better acquaintance, invited them, with their mother and brothers and a dozen or so of their youthful friends, to divert themselves at one of his country houses, where they spent a whole fortnight, and (as they confessed) in the most agreeable pastimes. Each day brought some fresh entertainment: they hunted, they hawked, they practised archery, they angled for gold-fish, or were rowed to the sound of music on the waters of their host's private canal, they picnicked in the ruined castles, of which he owned quite a number. Each day concluded, too, with banqueting, dancing, card-parties, theatricals; or would have concluded, had these young people felt any disposition to go to bed. They preferred, however, to sit up until morning, joking and teasing one another. *Blue Beard*, who had arrived at middle age, would have been grateful for a little more sleep than they allowed him, but showed himself highly complaisant and smiled at their pranks even when—their awe of him having worn off—they balanced a basin of water above his chamber door, to fall on his head and douch him, or sewed up his night-garments, or stuffed his bolster with the prickly cactus (an Eastern vegetable, of which he possessed whole avenues); nay, even when, for the same mischievous purpose, they despoiled his garden of an aloe which was due to blossom in a few days' time, after having remained flowerless for a century, he betrayed no chagrin but merely raised the wages of his head-gardener, heart-broken over the loss of a plant so economical in giving pleasure. In short all went so smoothly that the younger daughter began to find their host's beard not so blue after all.

She confided this to her mother. 'Dear mother,' she said, 'it is doubtless nothing more than my fancy, but his beard *does* seem to me to have altered in colour during the last ten days—a very little, of course.'

'Then you, too, have observed it!' the lady interrupted delightedly. 'My dearest child, you cannot imagine how your words relieve me! For a week past I have accused my eyesight of failing me, and myself of growing old.'

'Then you really think there *is* a change?' asked *Fatima*, at once doubtful and hoping.

'Indeed, yes. Ask yourself if it be reasonable to suppose that our eyes are playing a trick on both of us? Not,' her mother went on, 'that I, for my part, have any prejudice against blue. On the contrary, it is a beautiful colour, and considered lucky. The poets—you will have remarked—when they would figure to us the highest attainable happiness, select a blue flower or a blue bird for its emblem. Heaven itself is blue; and, at the least, a blue beard must be allowed to confer distinction.'

'A greyish-blue,' hazarded *Fatima.*

'A bluish-grey, rather,' her mother corrected her: 'that is, if I must define the shade as it appears to me.'

'And,' still hesitated *Fatima*, 'since it has begun to change, there seems no reason why it should not continue to do so.'

'My darling'—her mother kissed her—'that is precisely the point! Its colour is changing, you say. But for what reason? Obviously because he is in love; and what love has begun, love can carry to a conclusion. Nay, but put it on the ground of pity alone. Could a feeling heart set itself any task more angelic than to rescue so worthy a gentleman from so hideous an affliction—if affliction it be, which I am far from allowing?'

Fatima reflected on her mother's advice, but thought it prudent to consult her sister *Anne* and her step-brothers before coming to a decision which, once taken, must be irrevocable.

They listened to her very good-naturedly; though, to tell the truth, all three were somewhat jaded, having sat up all night at the card-tables,

They were rowed to the sound of music on the waters of their host's private canal.

They overran the house without loss of time.

And there, in a row, hung the bodies of seven dead women.

'You SHALL go in, and take your place among the ladies you saw there!'

The unhappy FATIMA cried up to her:-
'Anne, Sister Anne, do you see any one coming?'

Then BLUE BEARD roared out so terribly that he made the whole house tremble.

They overtook him just as he reached the steps of the main porch.

playing at ombre, quadrille, lasquenet, and Heaven knows what other games.

'My dear *Fatima*,' said her sister *Anne* with a little yawn, 'I congratulate you with all my heart on having made a discovery which, beyond a doubt and but for your better diligence, I should have had to make for myself before long.'

As for her step-brothers, they were in the best of humours at having won a considerable sum of money from their host by superior play ; and they answered her, quoting a proverb, that 'at nights all cats are grey, and all beards too,' and seemed to consider this very much to the point.

Fatima was greatly relieved by these assurances. On the evening before the company dispersed *Blue Beard* again sought a private interview and pressed his suit. She accepted him without further ado, and as soon as they returned to town the marriage was concluded.

They had been married little more than a month when *Blue Beard* came to his wife one morning, and told her that letters of importance had arrived for him: he must take a journey into the country and be away six weeks at least on a matter of business. He desired her to divert herself in his absence by sending for her friends, to carry them off to the country if she pleased, and to make good cheer wherever she was.

'Here,' said he, 'are the keys of the two great store-chambers where I keep my spare furniture; these open the strong-rooms of my gold and silver plate which is only used on state occasions; these unlock my chests of money, both gold and silver; these, my jewel coffers; and this is the master-key to all my apartments. But this little one, here, is the key of the closet at the end of the great gallery on the ground floor. Open all the others; go where you will. But into that little closet I forbid you to go; and I forbid it so strongly that if you *should* disobey me and open it, there is nothing you may not expect from my displeasure.'

Fatima promised to obey all his orders exactly; whereupon he embraced her, got into his coach, and was driven off.

Her good friends and neighbours scarcely waited for the young bride's invitation, so impatient were they to view all the riches of her grand house, having never dared to come while her husband was at home, because of his terrifying blue beard. They overran the house without loss of time, hunting their curiosity from room to room, along the corridors and in and out of closets and wardrobes, cabinets and presses; opening cupboards, ferreting in drawers, and still exclaiming over their contents as each new discovery proved more wonderful than the last. They roamed through the bedrooms and spent a long while in the two great store-chambers, where they could not sufficiently admire the number and beauty of the tapestries, beds, sofas, consoles, stands, tables, but particularly the looking-glasses, in which you could see yourself from head to foot, with their frames of glass and silver and silver-gilt, the finest and costliest ever seen. They ceased not to extol and to envy their friend's good fortune.

'If my husband could only give me such a house as this,' said one to another, 'for aught I cared he might have a beard of all the colours of the rainbow!'

Fatima, meanwhile, was not in the least amused by the sight of all these riches, being consumed by a curiosity even more ardent than that of her friends. Indeed, she could scarcely contain herself and listen to their chatter, so impatient she felt to go and open the closet downstairs. If only *Blue Beard* had not forbidden this one little thing! Or if, having reasons of his own to keep it secret, he had been content to take the key away with him, saying nothing about it! At least, if he wished to prove whether or not poor *Fatima* could rise above the common frailty of her sex—and he was, as we shall see, a somewhat exacting husband—he should have warned her. As it was, her curiosity grew and possessed her until at length, without even considering how uncivil it was to leave her guests, she escaped from them and ran down a little back staircase, in such haste that twice or thrice she tripped over her gown and came near breaking her neck.

When she reached the door of the closet she hesitated for a moment or so, thinking upon her husband's command, and considering what ill might befall her if she disobeyed it. While he uttered it his look had been extremely stern, and a blue beard —for after a month of married life she could no longer disguise from herself that it was still blue, or at any rate changing colour less rapidly than she or her mother had promised themselves—might betoken a harsh temper. On the other hand, and though she continued to find it repulsive, he had hitherto proved himself a kind, even an indulgent husband, and for the life of her she could not imagine there was anything unpardonable in opening so small a chamber. The temptation, in short, was too strong for her to overcome. She took the little key and, trembling, opened the door.

At first, shading her eyes and peering in, she could see nothing, because the window-shutters were closed. But after some moments she began to perceive that the light, falling through the shutters, took a reddish tinge as it touched the floor. So red it was—or rather, red-purple—that for a moment or two she supposed the closet to be paved with porphyry of that colour. Still, as she stared, and her eyes by degrees grew accustomed to the gloom, she saw—and moment by moment the truth crept upon her and froze her—that the floor was all covered with clotted blood. In the dull shine of it something horrible was reflected. . . . With an effort she lifted her eyes to the wall facing her, and there, in a row, on seven iron clamps, hung the bodies of seven dead women with their feet dangling a few inches above the horrible pool in which their blood had mingled. . . . Little doubt but these were the wives whom *Blue Beard* had married and whose throats he had cut, one after another!

Poor *Fatima* thought to die of fear, and the key, which she had pulled from the lock, fell from her hand. When she had regained her senses a little, she picked it up and locked the door again; but her hand shook so that this was no easy feat, and she tottered upstairs to recover herself in her own room. But she found it filled with her officious friends, who, being occupied with envy of her riches and having no reason to guess that, in a husband's absence, anything could afflict so fortunate a wife, either honestly ignored her pallor or hoped (while promising to come again) that they had not over-tired her by their visit.

They promised, too, to repeat their call very soon, at the same time inquiring how long her husband's journey might be expected to last. It was plain that they feared him, one and all. Half an hour ago she might have wondered at this.

They were gone at last. *Fatima*, drawing the

key from her pocket, now to her horror observed a dull smear upon it, and remembered that it had fallen at her feet on the edge of the pool of blood in the closet. She wiped it; she rubbed it on the sleeve of her robe; but the blood would not come off. In a sudden terror she ran to her dressing-room, poured out water, and began to soap the key. But in vain did she wash it, and even scrape it with a knife and scrub it with sand and pumice-stone. The blood still remained, for the key was a magic key, and there was no means of making it quite clean; as fast as the blood was scoured off one side it came again on the other.

She was still scouring and polishing, when a horn sounded not very far away. In her flurry she paid little heed to this, or to the rumble of wheels she heard approaching. Frightened though she was, she supposed that she had still almost six weeks in which to restore by some means the key to its brightness. But when the wheels rolled up to the porchway and came to a stop, and when the horn, sounding again, blew her husband's flourish, then indeed the poor lady's knees knocked together and almost sank beneath her. Hiding the key in the bosom of her bodice, she tottered forth to the head of the stairs, to behold *Blue Beard* himself standing beneath the lamp in the hall below.

He caught sight of her as she leaned over, clinging to the balustrade; and called up cheerfully that he had received letters on the road with news that his journey was after all unnecessary—the business he went about had been settled, and to his advantage. Still shaking in every limb, *Fatima* crept downstairs to give him greeting. She ordered supper to be prepared in haste; and while he ate, forced herself to ask a hundred questions concerning his adventures. In short she did all she could to give him proof that she was delighted at his speedy return.

Next morning, having summoned her to attend him on the terrace, he asked her to render back the keys; which she gave him, but with such a trembling hand that he easily guessed what had happened.

'How is this?' said he. 'Why is not the key of my closet among the rest?'

'I must have left it upstairs on my table,' said *Fatima*.

'Fetch it to me at once,' said *Blue Beard*. 'At once, and without fail.'

She went, and after a while returned, protesting that she could not find it.

'Go back and seek again,' commanded *Blue Beard*, dangerously calm.

After going backwards and forwards several times, she could pretend no longer, but brought him the key. *Blue Beard* examined it closely, and demanded—

'How came this blood upon the key?'

'I do not know,' answered poor *Fatima*, paler than death.

'You do not know!' cried *Blue Beard* in a terrible voice. 'But I know well enough. You have chosen to enter that closet. Mighty well, madam; since that poor room of mine so appeals to your fancy, your whim shall not be denied. You *shall* go in, and take your place among the ladies you saw there!'

Fatima flung herself at her husband's feet, and wept and begged his pardon with every sign of truly repenting her disobedience. She would have melted a rock, so beautiful and sorrowful she was; but *Blue Beard* had a heart harder than any rock.

'You must die, madam,' said he, 'and that presently.'

'Since I must die,' she answered, looking up at him with eyes all bathed in tears, 'grant me a little time to say my prayers.'

'I grant you,' replied *Blue Beard*, 'ten minutes, and not a second more.'

As she went from him, and through the house towards her own apartment, at the foot of the great staircase she met with her sister *Anne*, who (unaware of *Blue Beard's* return) had just arrived to pay her a visit.

'Ah, dear sister!' cried *Fatima*, embracing her. 'But tell me, oh, and for Heaven's sake, quickly! where are my brothers *Selim* and *Hassan*, who promised to come with you?'

'They are at home,' said *Anne*. 'They were detained at parade, and I have come ahead of them. I could wait for them no longer in my impatience to see you; but just as I was starting they arrived back from the parade-ground, and sent word that they will follow as soon as they have groomed their horses, and spend a happy day with you.'

'Alas!' sobbed *Fatima*, 'they will never see me alive in this world!'

'But what has happened?' asked her sister, amazed.

'He—*Blue Beard*—has returned. . . . Yes, and in a few minutes he has promised to kill me. But ah! ask me no questions—there is so little time left. Dear sister, if you love me, run upstairs and still up to the top of the tower, look if my brothers are not coming, and if you see them, give them a signal to make haste!'

Her sister *Anne* left her and ran up, up, to the roof of the tower; and from time to time as the minutes sped, the unhappy *Fatima* cried up to her:—

'*Anne, Sister Anne, do you see any one coming?*'

And *Sister Anne* answered her:—

'*I see nothing but the noon dust a-blowing, and the green grass a-growing.*'

By and by *Blue Beard*, who had pulled out his huge sabre, and was trying its edge on the short turf of the terrace, shouted to her:—

'Wife, your time is up. Come down, and at once!'

Then, as she made no answer, he shouted again, and as loudly as he could bawl: 'Come down quickly, or I will come up to you!'

'A moment—give me a moment longer!' she answered, and called softly to her sister: '*Anne, Sister Anne, do you see any one coming?*'

And *Sister Anne* answered: '*I see nothing but the noon dust a-blowing, and the green grass a-growing.*'

'Come down quickly,' shouted *Blue Beard*, 'or I will come up to you!'

'I am coming,' answered his wife; and again she cried: '*Anne, Sister Anne, do you see any one coming?*'

'I see,' answered *Sister Anne*, 'yonder a great cloud of dust coming.'

'Is it my brothers?'

'Alas! no, sister. I see a flock of sheep.'

'Will you not come down?' bawled *Blue Beard*.

'Just one moment longer!' entreated his wife, and once more she called out: '*Anne, Sister Anne, do you see nobody coming?*'

'I see,' she answered, 'yonder two Knights a-riding, but they are yet a great way off. . . . God be praised,' she cried a moment after, 'they are our brothers! I am waving my handkerchief to them to hasten.'

Then *Blue Beard* stamped his foot and roared out so terribly that he made the whole house tremble. The poor lady came down and, casting herself, all in tears and dishevelled, at his feet, clasped him by the ankles while she besought him for mercy.

'This shall not help you,' said *Blue Beard*. 'You must die!' Then, taking hold of her hair and twisting her head back, the better to expose her beautiful throat, he exclaimed: 'This be the lesson I read against curiosity, the peculiar vice of womankind, and which above all others I find detestable. To that most fatal habit all the best accredited religions, in whatever else they may differ, unite in attributing the first cause of all misfortunes to which the race is subject. . . .' In this strain he continued for fully three minutes, still grasping her hair with one hand while with the other he flourished his sabre.

As he ceased, poor *Fatima* looked up at him with dying eyes. 'Ah, sir!' she besought him, 'if this curiosity be, as you remind me, my worst sin, you will not be so cruel as to destroy me before I have confessed and asked pardon for it. Grant me, then, just one moment more to fix my thoughts on devotion!'

'No, no,' was his answer; 'recommend thyself to Heaven'; and he swung up his sabre to strike.

At that very instant there sounded so loud a knocking at the gate that he came to a sudden stop. His arm dropped as the gate flew open and two cavaliers ran in with drawn swords and rushed upon him. Loosing his hold upon *Fatima*, who sank fainting upon the grass, he ran to save himself, but the two brothers were so hot on his heels that, after pursuing him through the vineries and the orange-house, they overtook him just as he reached the steps of the main porch. There they ran their swords through his body, and, after making sure that he was dead, returned to their sister, who opened her eyes, indeed, as they bent over her, but had not strength enough to rise and embrace them.

Blue Beard had no heirs, and so his wife became mistress of all his estates. She employed a part of her wealth to marry her sister *Anne* to a young gentleman who had loved her a long while; another part to purchase captains' commissions for her two step-brothers; and the rest to marry herself to a very worthy gentleman who made her forget the short but unhappy time she had passed with *Blue Beard*.

MORAL

(For Curious Wives)

Wives should have one lord only. Some have reckon'd
In Curiosity t' enjoy a second.
But Scripture says we may not serve two masters,
And little keys have opened large disasters.

ANOTHER

(For Chastising or Correcting Husbands)

The very best sermon that ever was preach'd
Was a thought less effective the longer it reached.

CINDERELLA

OR THE LITTLE GLASS SLIPPER

ONCE upon a time there lived a gentleman who married twice. His second wife was a widow with two grown-up daughters, both somewhat past their prime, and this woman would have been the proudest and most overbearing in the world had not her daughters exactly resembled her with their fine airs and insolent tempers. The husband, too, had by his first wife a child of his own, a young daughter, and so good and so gentle that she promised to grow up into the living image of her dead mother, who had been the most lovable of women.

The wedding festivities were no sooner over than the stepmother began to show herself in her true colours. She could not endure the girl's good qualities, which by contrast rendered her own daughters the more odious. She put her to drudge at the meanest household work, and thus she and her precious darlings not only wreaked their spite but saved money to buy themselves dresses and finery. It was the child who scoured the pots and pans, scrubbed the floors, washed down the stairs, polished the tables, ironed the linen, darned the stockings, and made the beds. She herself slept at the top of the house in a garret, upon a wretched straw mattress, while her sisters had apartments of their own with inlaid floors, beds carved and gilded in the latest fashion, and mirrors in which they could see themselves from head to foot.

Yet they were so helpless, or rather they thought it so menial to do anything for themselves, that had they but a ribbon to tie, or a bow to adjust, or a bodice to be laced, the child must be sent for. When she came it was odds that they met her with a storm of abuse, in this fashion :—

'What do you mean, pray, by answering the

She used to creep away to the chimney-corner
and seat herself among the cinders.

They sent for the best hairdresser to arrange their hair.

And her godmother pointed to the finest of all with her wand.

She was driven away, beside herself with joy.

The KING'S son led her through the gardens, where the guests drew apart and gazed in wonder at her loveliness.

Whereupon she instantly desired her partner to lead her to the KING and QUEEN.

She made her escape as lightly as a deer.

The Prime Minister was kept very busy during the next few weeks.

bell in this state? Stand before the glass and look at yourself! Look at your hands—faugh! How can you suppose we should allow you to touch a ribbon, or even come near us, with such hands? Run downstairs, slut, and put yourself under the kitchen pump'—and so on.

'How can I help it?' thought the poor little drudge. 'If I do not run at once when the bell rings, they scold me for that. Yet they ring—both of them together sometimes—a minute after setting me to rake out a grate and sift the ashes. As for looking at myself in the glass, gladly would I do it if they allowed me one. But they have told me that if I had a glass I should only waste time in front of it.'

She kept these thoughts to herself, however, and suffered her ill-usage patiently, not daring to complain to her father, who would, moreover, have joined with the others in chiding her, for he was wholly under his wife's thumb; and she had enough of chiding already. When she had done her work she used to creep away to the chimney-corner and seat herself among the cinders, and from this the household name for her came to be *Cinder-slut*; but the younger sister, who was not so ill-tempered as the elder, called her *Cinderella*. They were wise in their way to deprive her of a looking-glass; for in truth, and in spite of her sorry rags, *Cinderella* was a hundred times more beautiful than they with all their magnificent dresses.

It happened that the King's son gave a ball, and sent invitations through the kingdom to every person of quality. Our two misses were invited among the rest, for they cut a great figure in that part of the country. Mightily pleased they were to be sure with their cards of invitation, all printed in gold and stamped with the broad red seal of the Heir Apparent; and mightily busy they were, discussing what gowns and head-dresses would best become them. This meant more worry for *Cinderella*, for it was she who ironed her sisters' linen, goffered their tucks and frills, pleated their wristbands, pressed their trimmings of old lace and wrapped them away in tissue paper. A score of times all this lace, piece by piece, had to be unwrapped, inspected, put away again; and after a trying-on, all the linen had to be ironed, goffered, crimped, or pleated afresh for them. They could talk of nothing but their ball dresses.

'For my part,' said the elder, 'I shall wear a velvet cramoisie trimmed *à l'Anglaise*'—for she had a passion for cramoisie, and could not perceive how ill the colour went with her complexion. 'I had thought of cloth-of-gold, but there's the cost of the underskirt to be considered; and underskirts seem to grow dearer and dearer in these days. What a relief,' she went on, 'it must be to have money and not be forced to set one thing against another!'

'I,' said the younger, 'must make shift with my old underskirt; that is, unless I can wheedle some money out of Papa'—for so, in their affection, they called their stepfather. '*Cinderella* can take out the worst stains to-morrow with a little eau-de-Cologne. I believe that, if she tries, she can make it look as good as new; and, at all events, it will give her something to do instead of wasting an afternoon. I don't pretend that I *like* wearing an old underskirt, and I hope to make dear Papa sensible of this; but against it I shall have the gold-flowered robe, on which I am determined, and my diamond stomacher, which is somewhat better than the common.'

'And I, of course,' said the elder, 'must wear my diamond spray. If only it had a ruby in the clasp instead of a sapphire! Rubies go so much better with cramoisie. . . . I suppose there is no time now to ask the jeweller to re-set it with a ruby.'

'But you don't possess a ruby, dear,' murmured her sister, who did possess one, and had no intention of lending it. 'And, besides, sapphires suit you so much better!'

They sent for the best milliner they could find, to build their mob-caps in triple tiers; and for the best hairdresser to arrange their hair; and their patches were supplied by the shop to which all the Quality went. From time to time they called up *Cinderella* to ask her advice, for she had excellent taste. *Cinderella* advised them perfectly, and even offered her services to dress their hair for them on the night of the ball. They accepted gladly enough.

Whilst she was dressing them one asked her: '*Cinderella*, would you not like to be going to the ball?'

'Alas! miss,' said *Cinderella*, 'you are making fun of me. It is not for the like of me to be there.'

'You are right, girl. Folks would laugh indeed to see *Cinder-slut* at a ball!'

Any one but *Cinderella* would have pinned on their mob-caps awry; and if you or I had been in her place, I won't swear but that we might have pushed in the pins just a trifle carelessly. But she had no malice in her nature; she attired them to perfection, though they found fault with her all the while it was doing, and quite forgot to thank her when it was done. Let it be related, in excuse for their tempers, that they had passed almost two days without eating, so eager were they and excited. The most of this time they had spent in front of their mirrors, where they had broken more than a dozen laces in trying to squeeze their waists and make them appear more slender. They were dressed a full two hours before the time fixed for starting. But at length the coach arrived at the door. They were tucked into it with a hundred precautions, and *Cinderella* followed it with her eyes as long as she could; that is to say, until the tears rose and blinded them.

She turned away weeping, back to the house, and crept into her dear chimney-corner; where, being all alone in the kitchen, she could indulge her misery.

A long while she sat there. Suddenly, between two heavy sobs she looked up, her eyes attracted by a strange blue glow on the far side of the hearth: and there stood the queerest lady, who must have entered somehow without knocking.

Her powdered hair was dressed all about her head in the prettiest of short curls, amid which the most exquisite jewels—diamonds, and rubies, and emeralds—sparkled against the firelight. Her dress had wide panniers bulging over a skirt of lace flounces, billowy and delicate as sea-foam, and a stiff bodice, shaped to the narrowest waist imaginable. Jewels flashed all over this dress—or at least *Cinderella* supposed them to be jewels, though, on second thoughts, they might be fireflies, butterflies, glowworms. They seemed at any rate to be alive, and to dart from one point to another of her attire. Lastly, this strange lady held in her right hand a short wand, on the end of which trembled a pale bluish-green flame; and it was this which had first caught *Cinderella's* eye and caused her to look up.

'Good evening, child,' said the visitor in a sharp clear voice, at the same time nodding kindly across the firelight. 'You seem to be in trouble. What is the matter?'

'I wish,' sobbed *Cinderella*. 'I wish,' she began again, and again she choked. This was all she could say for weeping.

'You wish, dear, that you could go to the ball; is it not so?'

'Ah, yes!' said *Cinderella* with a sigh.

'Well, then,' said the visitor, 'be a good girl, dry your tears, and I think it can be managed. I am your godmother, you must know, and in younger days your mother and I were very dear friends.' She omitted, perhaps purposely, to add that she was a Fairy; but *Cinderella* was soon to discover this too. 'Do you happen to have any pumpkins in the garden?' her godmother asked.

Cinderella thought this an odd question. She could not imagine what pumpkins had to do with going to a ball. But she answered that there were plenty in the garden—a whole bed of them in fact.

'Then let us go out and have a look at them.'

They went out into the dark garden to the pumpkin patch, and her godmother pointed to the finest of all with her wand.

'Pick that one,' she commanded.

Cinderella picked it, still wondering. Her godmother opened a fruit knife that had a handle of mother-of-pearl. With this she scooped out the inside of the fruit till only the rind was left ; then she tapped it with her wand, and at once the pumpkin was changed into a beautiful coach all covered with gold.

'Next we must have horses,' said her godmother. 'The question is, Have you such a thing as a mouse trap in the house?'

Cinderella ran to look into her mouse trap, where she found six mice all alive. Her godmother, following, told her to lift the door of the trap a little way, and as the mice ran out one by one she gave each a tap with her wand, and each mouse turned at once into a beautiful horse—which made a fine team of six horses, of a lovely grey, dappled with mouse colour.

Now the trouble was to find a coachman.

'I will go and see,' said *Cinderella*, who had dried her tears and was beginning to find this great fun, 'if there isn't such a thing as a rat in the rat trap. We can make a coachman of him.'

'You are right, dear,' said her godmother; 'run and look.'

Cinderella fetched her the rat trap. There were three large rats in it. The Fairy chose one of the three because of his enormous whiskers, and at a touch he was changed into a fat coachman.

Next she said: 'Go to the end of the garden; and there in the corner of the wall behind the watering-pot, unless I am mistaken, you will find six lizards. Bring them to me.'

Cinderella had no sooner brought them than her godmother changed them into six footmen, who climbed up at once behind the coach with their bedizened liveries, and clung on as though they had been doing nothing else all their lives.

The Fairy then said to *Cinderella*: 'Hey now, child! This will do to go to the ball with, unless you are hard to please.'

'Indeed, yes,' answered *Cinderella*. 'But how can I go, as I am, in these horrid clothes?'

'You might have given me credit for thinking of that too!' Her godmother did but touch her with her wand, and on the instant her rags were transformed into cloth of gold and silver, all bespangled with precious stones. She felt her hair creeping up into curls, and tiring and arranging itself in tiers, on the topmost of which a double ostrich feather grew from a diamond clasp that caught the rays of the old lady's wand and shot them about the garden, this way and that, making the slugs and snails crawl to shelter.

'But the chief mark of a lady,' said her godmother, eyeing her with approval, 'is to be well shod,' and so saying she pulled out a pair of glass slippers, into which *Cinderella* poked her toes doubtfully, for glass is not as a rule an accommodating material for slippers. You have to be measured very carefully for it.

But these fitted to perfection: and thus arrayed from top to toe, *Cinderella* had nothing more to do but kiss her godmother, thank her, and step into the coach, the six horses of which were pawing the cabbage beds impatiently.

'Good-bye, child!' said her godmother. 'But of one thing I must warn you seriously. I have power to send you thus to the ball, but my power lasts only until midnight. Not an instant beyond midnight must you stay there. If you over-stay the stroke of twelve, your coach will become but a pumpkin again, your horses will change back into mice, your footmen into lizards, and your ball dress shrink to the same rags in which I found you.'

Cinderella promised that she would not fail to take her departure before midnight : and, with that, the coachman cracked his whip and she was driven away, beside herself with joy.

In the royal palace, and in the royal gardens, over which shone the same stars which had looked down upon *Cinderella's* pumpkins, the ball was at its height: with scores and scores of couples dancing on the waxed floor to the music of the violins ; and under the trees, where the music throbbed in faint echoes, other scores of couples moving, passing and repassing, listening to the plash of the fountains and inhaling the sweet scent of the flowers.

Now, as the King's son walked among his guests, word was brought to him by his Chamberlain that a grand Princess, whom nobody knew, had just arrived and desired admission.

'She will not tell her name,' said the Chamberlain; 'but that she is a Princess and of very high dignity cannot be doubted. Apart from her beauty and the perfection of her address (of which your Royal Highness, perhaps, will allow me to be no mean judge), I may mention that the very jewels in her hair are worth a whole province.'

The King's son hastened to the gate to receive the fair stranger, handed her down from the coach, and led her through the gardens, where the guests drew apart and gazed in wonder at her loveliness. Still escorted by him she entered the ball-room, where at once a great silence fell, the dancing was broken off, the violins ceased to play—so taken, so ravished was everybody by the vision of this unknown one. Everywhere ran the murmur, 'Ah! how beautiful she is!' The *King* himself, old as he was, could not take his eyes off her, and confided to the *Queen* in a low voice that it was long since he had seen so adorable a creature.

All the ladies were busily studying her head-dress and her ball gown, that they might order the like next day for themselves, if only (vain hope!) they could find materials so exquisite and dressmakers clever enough.

The King's son took her to the place of honour, and afterwards led her out to dance. She danced so gracefully that all admired her yet the more. A splendid supper was served, but the young *Prince* ate nothing of it, so intent was he on gazing upon her.

She went and sat by her sisters, who bridled with pleasure at the honour. She did them a thousand civilities, sharing with them the nectarines and citrons which the *Prince* brought her; and still not recognising her, they marvelled at this, being quite unused (as they never deserved) to be selected for attentions so flattering.

The King's son now claimed her for another dance. It had scarcely come to an end when *Cinderella* heard the clock strike the quarter to twelve; whereupon she instantly desired her partner to lead her to the *King* and *Queen*. 'For I must be going,' she said.

'It is cruel of you to go so early,' he protested. 'But at least you will come again to-morrow and grant me many dances?'

'Is there to be another ball, then, to-morrow?' she asked.

'To-morrow, yes; and as many morrows as you wish, if only you will come.'

'Ah, if I could!' sighed *Cinderella* to herself: for she was young, and it seemed to her that she could never have enough of such evenings as this, though they went on for ever and ever.

The *Prince* led her to the daïs where sat the *King* and *Queen*. She made a deep reverence before them, a slighter but no less gracious one to the company, and withdrew. Although she had given no orders, her coach stood waiting for her. Slipping in, she was whisked home in the time it would take you to wink an eye.

She had scarcely entered the house, however, before she received a shock. For on the threshold of the kitchen, glancing down to make sure that her ball gown was not disarranged by this rapid journey, she perceived that it had vanished—changed back to the rags of her daily wear. But there, in the light of the hearth, stood her godmother, who smiled so pleasantly that *Cinderella* choked down her little cry of disappointment.

'Well, child? And how have you fared?'

'Godmama, I have never been so happy in all my life! And it is all thanks to you!' But after thanking her, *Cinderella* could not help confessing how she longed to go to the ball next evening. The King's son had begged her to come again, and oh! if she had been able to promise!

'As to that, child,' said her godmother, 'we will see about it when the time comes. But it has been lonely, keeping watch and sitting up for you. Will you not reward me by telling all about it?'

Cinderella needed no such invitation; she was dying to relate her adventures. She talked and talked, her godmother still smiling and questioning. For two hours, may be, she talked and was still recollecting a score of things to tell when her sisters' coach rumbled up to the gate, and almost at once there came a loud ring at the bell. She stared and rubbed her eyes, for at the first sound of it her godmother had vanished!

Cinderella ran and opened the door to her sisters. 'What a long time you have stayed,' said she, yawning, rubbing her eyes, and stretching herself as though she had just waked out of sleep.

(She had felt, however, no inclination at all to sleep since their departure !)

'If you had been at the ball,' said the elder sister, 'you would not have felt tired. One of the guests was the loveliest Princess—oh, the loveliest you ever could see! She showed us a thousand civilities. She gave us nectarines and citrons.'

Cinderella contained her joy. Upstairs, while she unplaited her sisters' hair and unlaced their bodices, she asked the name of the Princess. But they answered that no one knew her; that the King's son was wild about her, and would give everything in the world to discover who she was. *Cinderella* smiled. She no longer felt any temptation at all to be clumsy with the hairpins.

'Why then,' she said, 'she must be beautiful indeed. And she went away, you say, without telling her name? Is no one going to see her again?'

'As for that, she may come again to the ball to-morrow. I am told that the *Prince* begged it, almost with tears in his eyes. . . . For there is to be another ball to-morrow, and we are going!'

'Ah, heavens!' sighed *Cinderella*, how lucky

you are! Might I not just see her? Please, please, *Sister Caroline*, take me to-morrow—I could manage quite well if only you lent me your yellow gown which you wear every evening!'

'Hoity-toity!' snapped *Miss Caroline*. 'You cannot be awake. You must have been dreaming to some purpose if you see me lending my clothes to a nasty little Cinder-slut!'

Cinderella had quite well expected some such rebuff, and was glad enough to get it, for it would have been very awkward if her sister had been willing to lend the gown.

The next evening the two sisters were at the ball; and so was *Cinderella*, but in even finer attire than before. Her godmother had spared no pains, and as for the expense, that hardly needs to be considered when you can turn pumpkins into gilt coaches, cobwebs into Valenciennes lace, and beetles' wings into rubies, with the tap of a wand.

The King's son in his impatience flew to her coach door as soon as she arrived. Throughout the evening he never left her side, nor ceased to make pretty speeches; and she, pretty maid, was far from finding his behaviour tiresome—so far, indeed, that she forgot her godmother's warning. The end was, that in the midst of a dance she heard the stroke of a clock, looked up, was dismayed to find it the first stroke of twelve when she believed it yet an hour short of midnight, and made her escape as lightly as a deer. The *Prince* followed, but could not catch her. Only she dropped one of her glass slippers, which he picked up and treasured.

With the last stroke of twelve, coach and footmen had whisked away, and poor *Cinderella*, barefoot now as well as in rags, panted homeward over roads where the flints cut her until she bled, and the owls and great moths blundered out of the bushes against her face. To make matters worse, a thunderstorm broke before she had ran half the distance, and she arrived home in a terrible plight, muddy, drenched to the skin, and almost more dead than alive. In one thing only she was fortunate: she had outstripped her sisters, whose coach on the way home lost a wheel—and I have a suspicion that *Cinderella's* godmother had something to do with this misadventure too.

At all events when *Cinderella* opened the kitchen door the little lady stood as she had stood the night before, in the glow of the hearth, awaiting her.

'Well, child,' she said, frowning, yet the frown was not altogether unkindly, 'it is easily seen that you have forgotten my warning and have suffered for it. But what is *that* you are clutching?'

Poor *Cinderella* drew from under her bedraggled bodice a crystal slipper, fellow to the missing one. It was the one remnant of all her finery, and somehow, scarcely knowing why, she had hugged it to her while she ran and never let it slip in all her stumblings.

Her godmother gazed at her with a queer expression, that began by being a frown, yet in the end had certainly changed into a shrewd smile.

'You have been careless,' she said. 'Yet I am pleased to see that you have managed to keep, at any rate, one-half of your godmother's gift.' I think she meant by this that whereas all the rest of *Cinderella's* adornment had been contrived out of something other than it was, the two glass slippers had been really produced out of the Fairy's pocket.

They alone had not vanished at the stroke of midnight. 'But what has become of the other one?' her godmother asked.

Cinderella did not know for certain, but fancied that she must have dropped it in her hurry to escape from the palace.

'Yes, you are careless,' repeated the Fairy; 'but decidedly you are not unlucky.'

And with that she vanished, as the bell sounded announcing the sisters' return.

They were not in the best of humours, to begin with. *Cinderella* asked them if they had again found the ball enjoyable, and if the beautiful lady had been there. They told her yes; but that on the stroke of twelve she had taken flight, and so hurriedly that she had let fall one of her small glass slippers, the prettiest in the world, which the King's son had picked up. They added, that this indeed was the first cause of their delay; for, seeking their carriage, they had found the entry blocked, and the *Prince* in the wildest state of mind, demanding of the guards if they had not seen a Princess pass out. The guards answered that they had seen no one pass out but a ragged girl, who looked more like a country wench than a Princess. Amid this to-do, the sisters had with difficulty found their coach ; and then, within two miles of home, a wheel had come off and the coach had lurched over, in a thunderstorm, too ; and they had been forced to walk the rest of the way, the one with a bruised shoulder, and the other (which was worse) with a twisted ankle. But, after all, the dance had been worth these mischances and sufferings ; and, said they, harking back, the *Prince* was undoubtedly deep in love, for they had left him gazing fondly at the slipper, and little doubt—mysteriously as she chose to behave—he would make every effort to find the beautiful creature to whom it belonged.

They told the truth, too. For a few days after, the King's son had it proclaimed by sound of trumpet that he would marry her whose foot the slipper exactly fitted.

At first they tried it on the Princesses of the Court :

Then on the Duchesses :

Then on the Marchionesses :

Then on the Countesses and Viscountesses:

Then on the Baronesses:

And so on, through all the ladies of the Court, and a number of competitors, who, though they did not belong to it, yet supposed that the smallness of their feet was an argument that their parents had very unjustly come down in the world. The Prime Minister, who carried the glass slipper on a velvet cushion, was kept very busy during the next few weeks.

At length he called on *Cinderella's* two sisters, who did all they could to squeeze a foot into the slipper, but by no means could they succeed.

Cinderella, who was looking on and admiring their efforts, said laughingly:—

'Let me see if it will fit me.'

Her sisters began to laugh and mock at her, but the Prime Minister, who had come to make trial of the slipper, looked at *Cinderella* attentively, and seeing how good-looking she was, said that it was but just—he had orders to try it upon every one.

He asked *Cinderella* to sit down, and drawing the slipper upon her little foot, he saw that it went on easily, and fitted the foot like wax. Great was the astonishment of the two sisters; but it was greater when *Cinderella* pulled from her pocket the other little slipper and put it upon the other foot. On top of this came a rap at the door, and in walked the Fairy Godmother, who, by a touch of her wand upon *Cinderella's* clothes, made them still more magnificent than they had been before.

And now her two sisters knew *Cinderella* to be the same beautiful creature they had seen at the ball. They threw themselves at her feet, begging her pardon for all the ill-usage they had made her suffer. *Cinderella* raised and kissed them, saying that she forgave them with all her heart, and entreated them to be loving to her always.

They led her to the young *Prince*, arrayed as she was. He thought her lovelier than ever, and, a few days after, they were married. *Cinderella*, who was as good as she was beautiful, lodged her two sisters in the palace, and married them that same day to two great Lords of the Court.

Cinderella

MORAL

Better than wealth or art,
Jewels or a painted face,
It is when a natural heart
Inhabits its natural place
And beats at a natural pace.

ANOTHER

Yet youth that is poor of purse,
No matter how witty or handsome,
Will find its talents no worse
For a godmamma to advance 'em.

BEAUTY AND THE BEAST

ONCE upon a time, in a country a long way from here, there stood a flourishing city, full of commerce; and in that city lived a merchant so lucky in all his ventures that it seemed as if fortune waited on his wishes. But while enormously rich, he had a very long family of six sons and six daughters; and as yet not one of them was settled in life. The boys were too young to go out in the world; and the girls, who had everything at home the heart could desire, were in no hurry to risk a change by choosing a husband, although many rich and noble suitors paid court to them.

But one day an unexpected disaster brought this pleasant state of things to an end. Their house caught fire and was burnt to the ground; and with it perished not only the magnificent furniture, but the merchant's account books, bank notes, gold and silver, and the precious wares on which his wealth depended. Scarcely anything was saved.

This was but the beginning of their misfortunes. Their father, who up to now had prospered in everything he touched, lost in a very short while every ship he had upon the sea. Some were wrecked, others captured by pirates. His agents failed; his clerks in foreign countries proved unfaithful; and, in short, from the height of riches he suddenly fell into the direst poverty.

Nothing was left to him but one poor little country cottage, at least a hundred leagues from the city in which he had lived. In this he was driven to find refuge, and to this he carried off his family, who were in despair since the overthrow. The daughters especially could not endure the thought of dwelling in such a den (as they called it). At first they had felt sure that on hearing the news their suitors would be tripping one another up in haste to renew their offers of marriage. But in this they were soon undeceived. Their downfall was no sooner known than all these flattering wooers took to their heels in a troop. They fared no better with their intimate friends, who at once dropped their acquaintance. Nay, those to whom our merchant had formerly shown the greatest kindness were now the most eager to speak ill of him.

So nothing was left for this hapless family but to take their departure from the city and shut themselves up in the cottage, which stood in the depth of a dismal and almost trackless forest. No servants now to wait on them! The sons tilled the ground and swept out the farm sheds; and the daughters, dressed like country girls in coarse linen frocks, were forced to turn their delicate hands to the roughest employment and live on hard fare of which there was little enough.

Only the youngest daughter showed a brave heart. She had been despondent as any of them to begin with; but after weeping—as well she might—for her father's misfortunes, she recovered her natural gaiety, made the best of things, tried to forget how ungrateful the world had been, kept her father and her brothers amused with her cheerful wit, and after she had done her work, would sing and play. But her sisters would not join with her in making the best of things. 'It is very easy for you to be happy,' the eldest grumbled. 'You have low tastes and were born for this kind of life.' The fact is, they were all jealous of her because of her sweet temper and good looks. So beautiful, indeed, was this youngest sister that in the old days every one had agreed to call her *Beauty*—by that and by no other name she was known. Alone of them she might easily, in the first days of their ruin, have found a husband; but she could not think of this while she could be of use to help and console her family.

Two years passed, and there came news which seemed to offer a hope to escape. One of their father's ships, long supposed to be lost, had arrived in port with a rich cargo. The message further advised his return to the city with speed, or his agents might sell the goods too cheaply and he would lose his gains. So, whilst his children danced with joy at the news, the merchant set about preparing for his long journey.

In their transport his daughters loaded him with commissions for gowns and jewels it would have taken a fortune to buy. Only *Beauty* would not ask for anything. Her father, noting her silence, interrupted the others who still kept adding to their list of requirements.

'Well, *Beauty*,' he said, 'and what shall I bring home for you? Surely you, too, wish for something?'

'Dear father,' she answered, 'I wish for the most precious thing in the world; and that is to see you home again safe and sound.'

This answer covered the sisters with confusion, and vexed them so that one of them, speaking up for the others, said tartly: 'This small miss is putting on airs. She thinks, no doubt, she cuts a figure with her affected fine sentiments!'

Her father, however, was touched by her good feeling. Nevertheless he told her to choose something—'For,' said he, 'at your age it is only natural to like dresses and pretty presents.'

'Well, dear father,' said she, 'since you insist, I will beg you to bring me home a rose. I have not seen one since we came to live here, and I love roses.' In this way *Beauty* contrived to obey her father and yet to put him to no expense.

The day came for the merchant to embrace them all and bid them farewell. He made the best of his way to the great city; and arrived there to be met with a great disappointment. To be sure his vessel had come safely to port; but his partners, believing him dead, had taken possession of it and divided the cargo between them. To make good his claim he was forced to bring a number of tedious law-suits. He won them in the end; but only to find, after six months of trouble and expense, that he was almost as poor as when he started.

To make his misery complete he was forced to travel back in the winter, in the most inclement weather; so that by the time he reached the skirts of the forest he was ready to drop with fatigue. But reminding himself that his home was now not many leagues away, he called up what strength remained to him.

As he pushed on through the forest, night overtook him; and in the piercing cold, half buried —his horse and he—in the deep snow that hid every pathway, the poor merchant feared that his last hour had come. Not so much as a hut did he pass. The only shelter to be found was the trunk of a hollow tree; and there he cowered through the long night, kept awake by his hunger and the howling of the wolves. Nor did the day bring him much comfort: for thick snow lay everywhere, and not a path was to be seen. It was only after a weary search that he managed to recover his horse, which had wandered away and partly sheltered itself in another hollow tree. He mounted, and now in a little while discovered a sort of track which presently grew easier.

Following this, he found himself in an avenue of trees, at the entrance of which he halted and rubbed his eyes. For no snow had fallen in this avenue, and the trees were tall orange-trees, planted in four rows and covered with flowers and fruit; and here and there among the trees were statues, some of single figures, others of groups representing scenes of war, but all coloured like real life.

At the end of the avenue, straight in front of him, rose a magnificent castle in many terraces. The merchant rode around to the stable courtyard, which he found empty ; and there, with half-frozen hands, he unbridled and stabled his horse. Within the doorway he found a staircase of agate with balusters of carved gold. He mounted it and passed through room after room, each more splendidly furnished than the last. They were deliciously warm, too, and he began to feel his limbs again. But he was hungry ; where could he find some one to give him food ? Everywhere was silence ; and yet the place had no look of being abandoned. Drawing-rooms, bedchambers, galleries — all stood unlocked. . . . At last, tired of roaming, he came to a halt in an apartment where some one had lit a bright fire. A sofa drawn up cosily beside it, invited him to sit and warm his limbs ; and resting there, he closed his eyes and fell into deep and grateful slumber.

As weariness had sent him to sleep, so hunger awoke him. He opened his eyes and saw at his elbow a table with meats and wine upon it. He had been fasting for more than twenty-four hours, and lost no time in falling-to. He hoped that he might soon have sight of this most hospitable entertainer, whoever he might be, and an opportunity of thanking him. Still no one appeared; and now this good food did for him what fatigue had done before. He dropped off again into an easy slumber which lasted for four hours almost. Again awaking, he saw at his elbow another small table—of porphyry this time—upon which the unknown hands had set out a dainty meal of cakes, crystallised fruits and liqueurs. To this, too, he did justice. But, as the time still passed and no one appeared, he began to feel terrified, and resolved to search once more through all the rooms. . . . But still he found no one.

He was standing lost in thought, when of a sudden it came into his mind that some kindly power had perhaps prepared this palace of wonder for *him*, that it with all its riches might indeed be *his*. Possessed by this notion he once again made a tour of the rooms and took stock of their treasures, planning in his mind how he would divide them amongst his children, assigning this apartment to one and that to another, and whispering to himself

After she had done her work, would sing and play.

He had been fasting for more than twenty-four hours, and lost no time in falling to.

The good merchant let drop the rose and flung himself on his knees.

Soon they caught sight of the castle in the distance

She found herself face to face with a stately and beautiful lady.

These no sooner saw BEAUTY than they began to scream and chatter.

Ah! what a fright you have given me!
she murmured

what joy he would carry home after all from his journey. Then he went down into the garden, where—though it was the depth of winter—the birds were singing and the air breathed the scent of a thousand flowers.

'Surely,' he told himself, 'my daughters will be happy here and never desire any more to go back to the city. Quick! Let me saddle my horse at once and ride home with the news!'

The way to the stable was an alley fenced on either hand with palings, and over the palings hung great clusters of roses in bloom. They reminded him of his promise to *Beauty*. He plucked one, and was about to pluck a whole nosegay, when he was startled by a horrible noise behind him, and attempted to turn. But behind him stood a hideous *Beast* who was overtaking him and reaching out towards him.

'Who gave you leave to pluck my roses?' roared this monster. 'Was it not enough that I made you welcome in my palace and treated you kindly? And you show your gratitude by stealing my flowers! But your insolence shall not go unpunished!'

The good merchant, terrified no less by the sight of this *Beast* than by his threats, let drop the rose and flung himself on his knees.

'My Lord,' he cried, 'have pity on me! I am not ungrateful; but after all your kindness I could not guess that so small a thing would offend you.'

This speech did not at all abate the *Beast's* wrath. 'Hold your tongue, sir,' he commanded, 'if you can offer me nothing but flatteries and false titles. I am not "my lord." I am the *Beast*; and your words will not save you from the death you deserve.'

The merchant, although in fear of his life, plucked up courage to tell the monster that the rose which he had been bold to pluck was for one of his daughters, by name *Beauty*. Then, in hope either to delay the *Beast's* vengeance or to touch his compassion, he launched into the tale of all his misfortunes, and of his reasons for the journey, not forgetting to mention *Beauty* again and her request.

The *Beast* considered for a moment before answering him in a somewhat milder tone: 'I will forgive you; but only on condition that you give me one of your daughters. *Some one* must make amends for this trespass.'

'Heaven forgive me,' the merchant entreated, 'but how can I promise such a thing! Even were I cruel enough to purchase my life at the cost of a child, on what excuse could I bring her?'

'No excuse is necessary,' replied the *Beast* shortly. 'Whichever you bring must come here of her own free will, or not at all. Go home and try if there be one brave and loving enough to sacrifice herself to save your life. You seem to be an honest man. Give me your word to return here at the end of a month and bring whichever of your daughters you can persuade to come with you. If you can persuade none of them, you must come alone; and I warn you that, if you fail of it, I shall come and fetch you.'

What was the poor man to do? He promised, for he saw death staring him in the face; and having given his promise he hoped to be allowed to depart. But the *Beast* informed him that he could not go until next day.

'Then,' said he, 'at daybreak you will find a horse ready for you who will carry you home in less than no time. Now go and eat your supper, and await my commands.'

The merchant, more dead than alive, crept back to his rooms. There, before a blazing fire, he found a delicious supper spread, inviting him to eat. But so distraught was he, that no food, however delicious, could have tempted him had he not been afraid that the *Beast* might be hiding somewhere to watch him. In fear of this he forced himself to sit and taste of the dishes.

A loud noise in the next room warned him that the *Beast* was coming. Since he could not escape, he mustered what courage he could to conceal his terror, and faced about to the doorway.

'Have you made a good supper?' was the *Beast's* first question.

The merchant in humblest voice answered that, thanks to his host's kind attention, he had fared excellently well.

'I am paying you a visit,' said the *Beast*, 'to warn you again to be honest with your daughter. Describe me to her just as I am. Let her be free to choose whether she will come or no; but tell her that, her course once chosen, there can be no retreat, nor even reflection after you have brought her to me. To break faith then will avail nothing : she will but destroy you without winning her own release.'

Again the spirit-broken merchant repeated his promise.

The *Beast* appeared to be content at length. 'Retire to bed now,' he commanded, 'and do not get up to-morrow until you see the sun and hear a golden bell rung. Then, before starting, you will find breakfast laid for you here ; your horse will be standing ready saddled in the courtyard ; and you may carry back the rose to your daughter *Beauty* —as you call her. For the rest, I count on seeing you back in a month's time. So, farewell.'

The merchant, who dared not disobey a single one of these orders, retired to bed at once, though without any temptation to sleep ; and again, though he passed a wretched night, he was punctual to rise with the sun. A golden bell rang ; and prompt on the sound he found breakfast laid, still by unseen hands. After breakfast he went down to the stables, and on his way paused to pick up the rose, which lay in the alley where it had dropped from his hand.

It was fresh as ever, and smelt as sweetly as though it yet grew on the tree.

A few paces further on he found his horse standing ready saddled, with a handsome cloak of furs, far warmer than his own, lying across the saddle. He put it on and mounted, and now he had to wonder at yet another miracle. His horse set off at an incredible speed, so that before he could even turn in the saddle the palace had sunk out of sight.

Could the horse have felt the weight on the good man's mind, it had never made such a pace. But it took its own way, insensible to rein or bridle; nor halted until it reached the door of the cottage.

The merchant's sons and daughters had rushed out at his approach ; though it was not until he drew quite close that they recognised their father in this horseman superbly cloaked, with a rose at his holster, and mounted on a horse that travelled at such a speed. When they recognised him, they made sure that he brought the best of news. But the tears that trickled down his cheeks as he dismounted told them another story.

His first motion then was to pluck the fatal rose

from the pommel and hand it to *Beauty*, saying: 'Here is what you asked me to bring. You little know what it will cost you all.'

This, and his sorrowful look, gave the eldest daughter her cue. 'I was certain of it!' she said. 'Did I not say, all along, that to force a rose at this time of the year would cost you more than would have bought presents for all the rest of us? A rose, in mid-winter! and such a rose! There—one has only to look at it to see that you took good care *Beauty* should have her present, no matter at what cost to us!'

'It is all too true,' answered their father sorrowfully, 'that this rose has cost me dear—far dearer than all the presents you others begged of me. But the cost is not in money; for would to God I could have bought it with the last penny in my purse!'

His speech, you may be sure, excited their curiosity, and they gave him no rest until he had told the whole of his story. It left their hopes utterly dashed: and the daughters lamented their lot, while their brothers hardily declared that they would never allow their father to return to this accursed castle—they would march thither in a body and destroy the horrible *Beast* who owned it. But their father assured them that he had given his word and would rather die than break it.

Thereat the sisters turned upon *Beauty* and started to upbraid and rail against her.

'It is all your fault,' they declared; 'and this is what comes of your pretended modesty! Why could you not have asked for dresses and jewels as we did? Even if you could not get them, at least the demand would have cost nothing. But you chose to be singular—you, with your precious rose! and now our father must die, and we must all suffer through your affectation!'

Poor *Beauty* controlled her tears and answered them: 'Yes, I am to blame for all this, though, indeed, dear sisters, I did it innocently; for how could I guess that to ask for a rose in the middle of summer, as it was then, would give rise to all this misery? But what does that matter? Innocent or guilty, I cannot allow you to suffer for what was my fault; and so I will go back with our father to save him from his promise. That will be in a month's time, and in this little month, I beg of you, let us be happy together without reproaches.'

At first her brothers would not hear of any such sacrifice, and her father was equally set against it, until the sisters again fired up in their jealousy and accused him of being distressed only because it happened to be *Beauty* ; if another of his daughters (they hinted) had offered to pay this price for his life, he would have accepted it cheerfully enough !

Beauty closed this talk by saying firmly that, whether they wished it or not, she would go—'And who knows,' said she, forcing a brave smile, 'but this fate of mine, which seems so terrible, may cover some extraordinary and happy fortune ?' She said it merely to hearten them ; but her sisters, fancying her deluded by vanity and self-conceit, smiled maliciously and applauded. So their father gave way, and it was agreed that *Beauty* must go. For her part she desired only that the few days remaining to her might be as happy as possible ; and so, as they passed she spoke little of what was before her, and, if at all, only to treat it lightly and as a piece of good fortune. When the time drew near she shared up all her trinkets and little possessions with her sisters—for, badly as they had treated her, they were the only friends she had. Yet jealousy had made their hearts so wicked that when the fatal day arrived they actually rejoiced to hear the neighing of a horse which, punctually sent by the *Beast*, arrived at the door of the cottage.

The brothers would have rushed out and slain the beautiful animal ; but *Beauty*, mastering their anger with a few tender words, bade her father mount into the saddle ; and so, after bidding her sisters farewell with a tenderness that forced them to weep at the last, climbed to the pillion behind him quite as if she were setting out for a holiday. They were off! The horse seemed to fly rather than to gallop ; so smoothly that *Beauty* could scarcely feel the motion save by the soft wind that beat on her cheek. Soon they caught sight of the castle in the distance. Her father, less happy than she, again and again asked and begged her to alight and return—a most idle offer, for he had no real control of the reins. But *Beauty* did not listen, because her mind was made up.

Nevertheless, she was awed, and all the more when, as the fleet horse galloped up to the courtyard, they were met by a great salvo of guns and, as the echoes died away, by the sound of soft music within the palace.

The horse had come to a stop, by a flight of agate steps ; a light shone down these steps from a porchway within which the violins kept their throbbing. *Beauty* slipped down from the saddle, and her father, alighting after her, took her by the hand and led her to the chamber in which he had first supped ; where, sure enough, they found a cheerful fire and a score of candles lit and burning with an exquisite perfume, and—best of all—a table laid with the daintiest of suppers.

The merchant, accustomed to the ways of their host, knew that the supper was meant for them, and *Beauty* fell-to with a good appetite. Her spirits indeed were rising. There had been no sign of any *Beast* in all the many rooms through which she had passed, and everything in them had seemed to breathe of gaiety and good living.

But this happy frame of mind did not last long. They had scarcely finished supper when the *Beast* was heard coming through the distant rooms. At the sound—the heavy padding of his feet, the roar of his breath—*Beauty* clung to her father in terror, and had almost fainted against the arm which he flung around her. But when the *Beast* stood before her in the doorway, after a little shudder she walked towards him with a firm step, and, halting at a little distance, saluted him respectfully. This behaviour evidently pleased the *Beast*. After letting his eyes rest on her face for a while, he said, in a tone that might well have struck terror into the boldest heart (and yet it did not seem to be angry) :—

'Good evening, my good sir! Good evening, *Beauty*!'

The merchant was too far terrified to find his voice; but *Beauty* controlled hers and answered sweetly :—

'Good evening, *Beast*!'

'Have you come here of your own free will?' asked the *Beast*. 'And are you willing to let your father return and leave you here?'

Beauty answered that she was quite willing.

'Indeed? And yet what do you suppose will happen to you after he has gone?'

'Sir,' said *Beauty*, 'that is as it pleases you, and you only can tell.'

'Well answered,' replied the *Beast*; 'and since you have come of your own accord, you shall stay. As for you, my good sir,' said he to the merchant, 'you will take your departure at sunrise. The bell will give you warning; delay not to rise, eat your breakfast, and depart as before. But remember that you are forbidden ever to come within sight of my palace again.'

Then, turning to *Beauty*, he said :—

'Take your father into the next room, and choose between you everything you think will please your brothers and sisters. You will find there two travelling trunks: fill them as full as they will hold.'

Sorrowful as she was at the certainty of losing her father so soon and for ever, *Beauty* made ready to obey the *Beast's* orders, and he left them as he had come, saying :—

'Good night, *Beauty*! Good night, good sir!'

When they were alone, *Beauty* and her father went into the next room, which proved to be a store-chamber piled with treasures a king and queen might have envied. After choosing and setting apart in heaps,—one for each of her sisters,—the most magnificent dresses she could find, *Beauty* opened a cupboard which had a door of crystal framed in gold, and stood for a moment dazzled by the precious stones that lay piled on every shelf. After choosing a vast number and adding them to her heaps, she opened yet another wardrobe and found it full of money in gold pieces. This set her pondering.

'I think, father,' she said, 'that we had better empty these trunks again, and fill them with money. For money can always be turned to account, whereas to sell these precious stones you would have to go to some jeweller, who very likely would cheat you, and perhaps be suspicious of them. But with these pieces of gold you can buy land, houses, furniture, jewels—what you will—and no one will ask any questions.'

Her father agreed. Yet he first of all tried to make room for the money by emptying out the few things he had packed for himself. But this was no good : for it seemed that the trunks were made in folds which opened the wider the more he put in. Somehow the more they packed, the more room there seemed to be, and they ended by replacing all the dresses and precious stones they had taken out.

But now the trunks were so heavy that an elephant would have sunk under them.

'It is all a cheat!' cried the merchant. The *Beast* is mocking us, and only pretended to give us these things, knowing that I could not carry them away.'

'Wait a little,' advised *Beauty*. 'That would be a sorry jest, and I cannot help thinking that the *Beast* is honest; and that since he offered these gifts he will find you also the means to carry them. The best thing we can do is to strap up the trunks and leave them ready here.'

So they did this and went back to the little room, where to their amazement they found a breakfast laid on the table. For a moment they could scarcely believe that the night had flown by whilst they were occupied in ransacking the treasure chamber and packing the trunks. But, glancing at the windows, they saw that day was indeed breaking; and presently a bell sounded, warning the merchant to eat quickly and depart.

He finished his meal, and they went down together to the courtyard, where two horses stood ready—the one laden with the two trunks, the other saddled for the merchant to ride. And now *Beauty* and her father would fain have spent a long time in bidding one another farewell. But the two horses neighed and pawed the ground so impatiently that he was afraid to linger. Tearing himself from his daughter's arms he mounted in haste, and could scarcely turn to say good-bye before both horses sprang away swift as the wind and he was lost to sight in an instant.

Poor *Beauty* ! She gazed and gazed through her tears, and so mounted the stairs sorrowfully back to her own chamber. On reaching it she felt herself oppressed with sleepiness, for she had passed the night without undressing, and, moreover, for a month past her sleep had been broken and haunted with terrors. So, having nothing better to do, she went to bed, and was nestling down in the perfumed sheets when her eyes fell on the little table by the bedside. Some one had set a cup of hot chocolate there, and, half asleep, she reached out her hand for it and drank it ; whereupon her eyes closed and she fell into a delicious slumber, such as she had not known since the day when her father brought home the fatal rose.

She dreamed that she was walking alongside an endless canal, the banks of which were bordered with tall orange-trees and myrtles in flower. There, as she wandered disconsolately lamenting her fate, of a sudden a young *Prince* stood before her. He was handsome as the God of Love in picture-books, and when he spoke it was with a voice that went straight to her heart. 'Dear *Beauty*,' he said, 'you are not so unfortunate as you suppose. It is here you shall find the reward of your goodness, denied to you elsewhere. Use your wits to find me out under the disguise which hides me—that is, if as I stand here now you find me not altogether contemptible. For I love you tenderly—you alone—and in making me happy you can attain to your own happiness. Beloved, never distrust your own true heart, and it shall lead you where the heart has nothing left to desire!' So saying, the charming apparition knelt at her feet, and again besought her to accept his devotion and become mistress over all his life.

'Ah! What can I do to make you happy?' she asked earnestly.

'Only be grateful,' he answered, 'and do not

believe all that your eyes would tell you. Above all, do not abandon me until you have rescued me from the cruel sufferings I endure.'

With that the dream melted away, but only to be succeeded by another. She found herself face to face with a stately and beautiful lady; and the lady was speaking to her with dignity, yet most kindly.

'Dear *Beauty*,' she said, 'do not grieve for what you have left behind; a far higher destiny lies before you. Only, if you would deserve it, beware of being misled by appearances.'

Beauty found her dreams so agreeable that she was in no hurry at all to awake, and even when her eyes opened to the daylight she had more than half a mind to close them again. But a clock, chiming out her own name twelve times, warned her that it was midday and time to get up. She rose, therefore, and found her dressing-table set out with brushes and combs and everything she could want; and having dressed carefully, and with a lightness of heart for which she found it hard to account, she passed into the next room and found her dinner on the table.

Dinner does not take very long when you are

all by yourself. *Beauty*, when she had eaten enough, sat down on a sofa and began to think of the handsome youth she had seen in her dream. 'He told me I could make him happy. Why, then, it must be that the horrible *Beast*, who appears to be master here, is keeping him a prisoner. How can I set him free? . . . They both warned me not to trust to appearances. It is all very puzzling. . . . But one thing is clear at any rate, that I am very silly to be vexing my head over a dream. I will forget all about it, and look for something to do to amuse myself.'

She sprang up, and started to make a tour of discovery through the many rooms of the palace. They were even grander than she had expected. The first she entered was lined with mirrors from floor to ceiling, where she saw herself reflected on every side. The next thing to catch her eye was a bracelet, hanging from one of the chandeliers. Set in the bracelet was a gold locket, and opening this she was startled indeed; for it contained a portrait in miniature of the gallant youth she had seen in her dream. She could not be mistaken; so closely were his features engraved on her memory

—yes, and, it may be, on her heart. She slipped the bracelet on her wrist, without stopping to think that it did not belong to her, and went on to explore further. She passed into a long picture gallery, and there again she met the *Prince's* face. It smiled down at her, this time from a life-sized portrait, and it seemed to smile so wistfully that she caught herself blushing.

From the gallery her steps had led her to a chamber filled with instruments of music. *Beauty* was an accomplished musician; so, sitting down, she amused herself by tuning and trying over one instrument after another; but she liked the harp best because that went best with her voice.

Leaving the music-room at length, she found herself in a long chamber like the picture gallery, but lined with books. It held an immense library; and *Beauty*, ever since she had lived in the country, had been forced to do without reading, for her father had sold all his books to pay his debts. Now, as her eyes travelled along the shelves, she knew she need never have any fear that time would pass heavily here. The dusk was gathering before she had half-studied even the titles of the thousands of volumes ; and numbers of candles, waxen and scented, in chandeliers with lustres of diamonds and rubies, were beginning to light themselves in every room.

In due time *Beauty* found supper laid and served for her, with the same good taste and orderliness as before, and still she had seen no living face. What did this matter ? Her father had warned her that she would be solitary ; and she was beginning to tell herself that she could be solitary here without much discomfort, when she heard the noise of the *Beast* approaching. She could not help trembling a little ; for she had not yet found herself alone with him, and knew not what would happen—he might even be coming to devour her. But when he appeared he did not seem at all ferocious.

'Good evening, *Beauty*,' he said gruffly.

'Good evening, *Beast*,' she answered gently, but shaking a little.

'Do you think you can be content here ?' he asked.

Beauty answered politely that it ought not to be hard to live happily in such a beautiful palace.

After this they talked for an hour, and in the course of their talk *Beauty* began to excuse many things in the *Beast*—his voice, for example. With such a nose how could he help roaring through it? Really, he appeared to be wanting in tact rather than purposely terrible; though, to be sure, this want of tact terrified her cruelly, when at length he blurted out:—

'Will you be my wife, *Beauty*?'

'Ah! I am lost!' thought *Beauty*. The *Beast* could not be so dull-witted after all, for, though she kept the cry to herself, he answered quickly, and just as if she had uttered it aloud:—

'Not at all. I wish you to answer just "yes" or "no."'

'Oh! no, *Beast*.'

'Very well, then,' said this tractable monster. 'Since you will not, I had best be going. Good night, *Beauty*.'

'Good night, *Beast*,' answered *Beauty*, relieved of her fright. She felt sure now that he did not mean to hurt her, and as soon as he had taken his leave she went off to bed, and was asleep in no time.

But almost as quickly she was dreaming, and in her dream at once she saw her unknown lover standing beside her, handsome as ever, but more sorrowful than before.

'Dear *Beauty*,' he said, 'why are you so cruel to me? I love you the better for being so stubborn, and yet it lengthens out my misery.'

She could not understand this at all. Her dream wavered and it seemed to her that he took a hundred different shapes in it. Now he had a crown between his hands and was offering it to her; now he was kneeling at her feet; now he smiled, radiant with joy; and again he buried his head in despair and wept till the sound of his sobbing pierced her heart. Thus, in one aspect or another, he was with her the night through. She awoke with him in her thoughts, and her first act was to unclasp the locket on her wrist and assure herself that the miniature was like him. It certainly was the same face, and his, too, was the face that smiled down from the larger portrait in the gallery. But the face in the locket gave her a more secret joy and she unclasped and gazed on it again and again.

This morning she went down into the gardens, where the sun shone inviting her to ramble. They were beyond imagination lovely. Here stood a statue showered over with roses; there fountain on fountain played and threw a refreshing spray so high in the air that her eyes could scarcely reach to its summit. But what most surprised her was that every nook and corner recalled those she had seen in her dreams with the unknown *Prince* standing beside her. At length she came to the long canal with the oranges and myrtles in the shade of which she had first seen him approach. It was the very spot, and she could no longer disbelieve that her dreams were real. She felt sure, now, that he must somehow be imprisoned here, and resolved to get at the truth that very evening, should the *Beast* repeat his visit.

Tired at length of wandering, she returned to the palace and discovered a new room full of materials for work to engage the most idle—tape-bags, distaffs and shuttles, frames for tapestry, ribbons to make into bows, silks for embroidery, scissors, and thimbles. Beyond this needlework room a door opened upon the most wonderful sight of all—an aviary full of the rarest birds, yet all so tame that they flew to *Beauty*, and perched themselves on her shoulders.

'Dear birds,' she said, 'I wish you were closer to my own room, that I might sit and hear you singing.'

She had scarcely said it when, opening a door beyond the aviary, she found herself in her own chamber—yes, her very own!—which she had thought to be quite on the other side of the building. The door, when she came to examine it, had a shutter which could be opened to hear, and closed again when she grew tired of it. This aviary opened on another inhabited by parrots, parroquets, and cockatoos. These no sooner saw *Beauty* than they began to scream and chatter; one wishing her 'Good morning,' another inviting her to luncheon, while a third yet more gallant cried 'Kiss me! Kiss me!' Others again whistled airs from grand opera or declaimed pieces of poetry by the best authors. It was plain that in their several ways they all had the same object—to amuse her.

Beyond the aviaries lay a monkey house. Here

were apes of all sorts—Barbary apes, mandarin apes, apes with blue faces, baboons, marmosets, chimpanzees—and all came frisking about her, bowing and scraping, to show how much they appreciated the honour of this visit. To celebrate it they stretched a tight-rope and danced, and threw somersaults with an agility which *Beauty* found highly diverting; and yet she could not help sighing that none of these animals were able to tell her news of her unknown *Prince Charming*. She patted and made much of them, however, and asked if some of them would be kind enough to come with her and keep her company.

At once, and as if they had only been waiting for this command, two large she-apes in sweeping court-dresses stepped to her side and became her maids of honour; two brisk little marmosets volunteered for pages and held up her train; while an affable baboon, his face wreathed with smiles, bowed, presented a gloved hand, and begged leave to squire her. With this singular escort *Beauty* marched back to luncheon, and while she ate it the birds piped and fluted around her for accompaniment to the parrots, who lifted up their voices and chanted the latest and most fashionable tunes. Nay more; the meal was no sooner ended than the apes begged her to allow them to entertain her with a light comedy; which (leave being granted) they proceeded to act in a highly creditable manner and with appropriate dumb-show, while the parrots spoke the words from the wings very distinctly and in accents that exactly conformed with the various parts. At the close one of the actors advanced, laid his hand on his heart and—still with the parrot for interpreter—thanked *Beauty* for the indulgence she had shown to their poor efforts.

That night again, after supper, the *Beast* paid her his accustomed visit. He put the same questions, and received her answers as before; and, as before, the conversation ended by his taking leave of her with a 'Good night, *Beauty*.' The two she-apes, as ladies-in-waiting, thereupon undressed their mistress and saw her to bed. Before leaving they thoughtfully opened the window-shutter, that the soft night-warbling of the birds might soothe her to sleep and dream of her lover.

In this fashion day followed day, and still

Beauty found plenty to amuse her. At the end of a week she made the most wonderful discovery of all. There was one large room which she had entered but once, because it seemed to her rather dull, and dark too. It was empty; and although it had four windows in each wall, but two of them admitted any light. One day, as she passed the door, the fancy took her to open one of these windows. She stepped in and drew the shutter, when to her astonishment it opened, not upon daylight at all, but what seemed to be a dim hall lit only by a glimmer, distant and faint, behind the chinks of a thick curtain at the further end. She was wondering what this might mean, when the curtain went up and in a sudden flood of light she found herself gazing, as from a box, into a theatre crowded from floor to ceiling, and with an audience brilliant in dresses and jewels.

An orchestra played the overture, and gave place to the actors—real actors this time, not apes and parrots. The play was charming, and *Beauty* in ecstasy with every scene of it. When the curtain fell she still lingered in her box, hoping to see the fashionable crowd disperse; but somewhat to her chagrin the lights went out almost at once and the theatre was dark again. Still it had been very pleasant, and she promised herself to become a constant playgoer.

That evening when the *Beast* paid his visit, she told him all about the comedy. 'Eh? You like that sort of thing, do you?' asked the monster. 'Well, you shall have as much of it as you like. You are so pretty.' *Beauty* could not help smiling inwardly at his clumsy compliments. But she smiled no longer when he put to her once again his blunt question :—

'*Beauty*, will you be my wife?'

'No, *Beast*,' she answered as before; but she was really beginning to get frightened, he was so gentle and so persistent. She sat up so long thinking over this that it was almost daylight before she closed her eyes in bed; and at once, as if impatient at being kept waiting, the lover of her dreams presented himself. Perhaps for this reason he was not in the best of tempers; at any rate he taxed her with being moody and discontented.

'I should be happy enough,' she answered, 'if

the *Beast* did not pester me so. I—I almost think, by his foolish compliments, that he would like me to marry him.' *Beauty* expected her dream-lover to show some jealousy at this; seeing that he merely stood glum, she went on, 'Would you really be content if I married him? . . . but alas! no; were he as charming as he is hideous, you know that I love you and can never love any one else.' By all rights the *Prince* should have been in raptures at this avowal; but all his answer was: 'Dearest, love him who best loves you. Do not be led astray by appearances, and so you will free me from captivity.' This was not only puzzling; it seemed to *Beauty* to be just a little selfish. 'At least,' she said, 'tell me what to do! Since liberty appears to be your first wish, believe me, I would liberate you at any sacrifice, if only I knew how.' But this was what she could never discover; and because of it her nights now, though she longed for them, troubled her more than her days.

Her days passed pleasantly enough, and still in fresh discoveries. One by one in their turn she opened the windows of the great hall, and they revealed:—

First, a grand performance of Opera ; and she listened not to the singers only, but to the murmur of the audience between the acts. To listen to this and to gaze on human faces, gave her an inexpressible pleasure.

Next, a great Fair in progress. When first she looked the throng had not arrived and she inspected the booths at leisure, with their various wares. As the spectators drifted in, the drums began to beat, the hobby horses to revolve, the showmen to shout, the marionettes to perform in their little theatre. It was ravishing.

After this she beheld a fashionable promenade, with a richly dressed crowd passing, re-passing, exchanging good-days, remarking how superb was the weather, and pausing to con and criticise the shop windows to right and left.

The next spectacle was a gaming-room, with the players seated at their cards or roulette, the croupiers spinning the ball or raking the money. *Beauty*, with nothing to stake, had leisure to observe their faces, and how sadly some left the tables who had come smiling with money in their pockets. She saw, too, that some were being cheated; and it vexed her, because she could not warn them.

Next, she was gazing at the Royal Palace, where the King and Queen were holding a reception. She saw ambassadors with their wives, lords and ladies and state counsellors; and watched them as they passed by the throne making their lowest bows.

A water picnic followed this. The boats lay moored alongside a bank where the merry-makers sat or lounged and talked to the sound of lutes.

The picnic ended in a ball, with violins playing and couples advancing and retreating on the waxed floor that shone in the light of a thousand candles. Oh, how *Beauty* longed to be one of the dancers!

But perhaps the last window gave her the most pleasure. For through it she was able to see the whole world at one gaze and all that was going on in it. State embassies, royal weddings, coronations, pageants, armies, revolutions, sieges, pitched battles —she could sit at her ease and watch them all, which was far more amusing than it is to read about them in a newspaper.

She ought, you will say, to have been happy as the day was long. But no : a life becomes flat and stale which is a perpetual round of pleasure and leaves nothing to sigh or to hope for. *Beauty* began to long for a sight of her father and her brothers and sisters. She concealed this for a while, however, and turned her thoughts to what was more pressing ; for she could not beg leave to go home until something had been done to rescue her dear Unknown and restore him to liberty. The *Beast* alone (she reflected) could tell her the secret ; and she thought to herself that, being himself so blunt of speech, he would forgive some bluntness in her. So one evening she asked him point-blank : '*Beast*, are we alone in this palace, with nobody but ourselves ? '

'Of course we are,' he answered gruffly ; but the question appeared in some way to sting him, for almost at once he rose and bade her good night.

Now *Beauty*, whatever else she thought of the *Beast*, had by this time learnt to trust him for honest. It was a dreadful disappointment, therefore, to be forced to believe on his word that her

Prince Charming had no existence outside of her fancy. She slept ill that night. In her dream she was wandering again and sorrowfully alongside the canal when her lover appeared and took her hands between his while he scanned her face all bathed in tears.

'What has gone wrong, dear *Beauty*?' he demanded. 'Why are you in this distress? . . . Ah, it is the *Beast* who persecutes you! But, never fear, you shall be delivered here and now from his attention'—and with these words the *Prince* snatched out a dagger and rushed on the monster, who now for the first time came into the dream, advancing slowly down the bank of the canal. Strange to say, he offered no resistance even when the dagger almost touched his throat. But *Beauty*, whom an unseen power held back as she would have run to prevent the murder, on the instant found voice to cry, 'Stay! Stay, rash fool! or kill me before you kill him who has been my best friend!' 'Friend?' answered back the *Prince*, still with his dagger lifted; 'and am I no more than that?' 'You are an unfaithful one, at any rate,' persisted *Beauty*; 'if, knowing well that I would lay down my life for you, you would take the life of one who has done me so much kindness.' But while she pleaded the figures wavered in her dream, still struggling together, and vanished, giving place to the same stately lady she had seen in her former vision. 'Courage, *Beauty*!' said this fresh phantom; 'your happiness is not far off, if only you will go your own way and trust not to appearances.'

This dream left *Beauty* so uneasy that next day she opened one window after another to cure her restlessness; and, when this would not do, all the windows together; but still in vain. That night, when the *Beast* paid his usual visit, he detected almost at once that she had been weeping, and demanded the reason.

'Ah, sir,' said *Beauty*, 'if only I might go home!'

'You wish to go home?' The *Beast's* face turned pale—which, for such a face, was no easy matter. He staggered backwards with a deep sigh, or rather, a roar of grief. 'Ah, *Beauty*, *Beauty*! Would you desert a poor *Beast*? What more can I do to make you happy? Or is it because you hate me, that you wish to be gone?'

'No, *Beast*,' answered *Beauty* gently; 'I do not hate you, and I should be very sorry never to see you again. But I do long to see my own people. Let me go home for two months only, and I promise to come back and stay with you for the rest of my life.'

The *Beast* had fallen flat and lay along the carpet at her feet. His eyes were closed, and for some while his heavy sighs alone told her that he was neither dead nor in a swoon. By and by he lifted his head :—

'I can deny you nothing,' he said sadly. 'But no matter, though it cost me my life. . . . In the room next to your bedroom you will find four chests : fill them with everything you would like to take with you. Be sure to keep your word ; for if you break it and come back to find your poor *Beast* dead, you will be sorry when it is too late. Come back at the end of two months and you will find me alive ; and to come back you will not need chariot or horses. Only say good-bye, that night, to your father, and brothers, and sisters ; and, when you are in bed, turn this ring round on your finger and say firmly : "I wish to go back to my palace and see my *Beast* again." That is all. Good night, *Beauty!* Sleep soundly, and in good time you shall see your father once more.'

As soon as he was gone *Beauty* set to work to fill the four boxes with all the riches and finery that heart could desire. She filled them to the brim; and then, tired out, she went to bed. But for a long while she could not close her eyes for excitement. It was not until close upon sunrise that sleep visited her and, with it, another dream. In this dream she saw her beloved Unknown stretched at full length on a bank of turf. His face was hidden, and she could hear that he was sobbing. But when, touched by the sight of his grief, she drew near to console him, he lifted his face to her and said:—

'Cruel *Beauty*, how can you ask what ails me? when you are leaving me, and your going is my death warrant!'

'But, dearest *Prince*,' said *Beauty*, 'I am only going to tell my father and brothers and sisters that I am well and happy. In a short while I shall be back, never to leave you again. . . . But, for that matter,' she went on as a new thought struck her, 'why should we be separated at all? I will put off my going for another day, and to-morrow I will beg the *Beast* to let you go with me. I am sure he will not refuse.'

'I can only go with you, if you promise me never to come back,' replied the *Prince*. 'And, after all, when you have once delivered me, why should we ever come back? The *Beast* will be hurt in his feelings and very angry no doubt; but by that time we shall be beyond his power.'

'You forget,' *Beauty* reminded him sharply, 'that I have promised him to return, and that, moreover, he says he will die of grief if I break my word.'

'And what if he does?' demanded her lover. 'Is not your happiness worth more than the life of a monster? Of what use is he in the world except to frighten folks out of their wits?'

'Ah, you do not understand!' cried *Beauty*. 'This monster—as you call him—is only a monster in his face, and through no fault of his. He has the kindest heart in the world, and how could I be so ungrateful after all he has done for me!'

'I believe,' said her lover bitterly, 'that if you

saw us fighting, of the two you would rather let me perish than this *Beast* of yours.'

Beauty told him that he was cruel and unjust, and begged him to talk of something else. She set the example, too. Seeing that he was piqued and proud, she addressed a long speech to him, full of endearments, to win him back to a good humour, and was growing astonished at her own eloquence when, in the middle of it, she awoke.

Her last words seemed to mingle with the sound of familiar voices. She sprang out of bed and drew her curtain. . . . It was very strange! As the sunlight poured in she saw that she was in a room much more poorly furnished than that in which she had fallen asleep. She dressed in haste, and opening the door, found that the next room too was like no apartment in the *Beast's* palace. But at her feet stood the four chests she had packed overnight; and, while she marvelled, again she heard a voice talking, and ran towards it. For it was her father's.

She rushed out and fell into his arms. He, poor man, stared at her as though she had sprung from another world, and the others were no less astonished. Her brothers embraced her with transports of joy, while her sisters—who, to tell the truth, had not overcome their jealousy—pretended to be quite as glad. They plied her with a thousand questions, which she answered very good-naturedly, putting aside her own impatience ; for she too had a number of questions to ask. To begin with, this house of theirs was not the cottage in which she had left them, but a fine new one her father had been able to buy with the *Beast's* presents. If not wealthy, he was in easy circumstances ; with the bettering of their fortunes his sisters had found other wooers and were soon to be married ; and altogether *Beauty* had the satisfaction of knowing that she had at least brought prosperity back to her family. 'As for you, my dearest child,' said the merchant, 'when your sisters are married, you shall keep house for your brothers and me, and so my old age will be happy.'

This was all very well, but *Beauty* had to tell her father that she must leave him again in two months' time ; whereat he broke out into lamentations. 'Dear father,' said the sensible girl, 'it is good of you to weep ; but it is useless, and I would rather have your advice, which is sure to be useful.' Thereupon she told him all the story. Her father considered for a while, and then said :—

'I can only give you the same counsel that, by your own admission, you are always receiving from these phantoms of your dreams. "Do not trust to appearance," they say, and "Be guided by your heart's gratitude"; and they tell you this over and over again. What can it mean, child, but one thing? The *Beast*, you say, is frightful. His appearance is certainly against him. Then judge him rather by the gratitude which you certainly owe him. It is plain that he has a good heart—"handsome is as handsome does"—it is clear to me that these phantoms would have you say "Yes" to the *Beast*, and I too advise you to consent.'

Beauty saw the wisdom of this and knew very well that her father was counselling her for the best. Nevertheless it needed something more than this to reconcile her with marrying a monster, and she felt relieved at the thought that for two whole months she could put off deciding. Strange to say, as the days went by and the time of her departure drew nearer, she found herself looking forward to it rather than repining. For one thing distressed her and spoilt all her happiness—she never dreamed at all now.

The days went by, and as they drew to an end her brothers and even her father (forgetting his former good counsel) employed all persuasions to hinder her departure. But her mind was made up; and when the two months were passed she was resolute on everything but the hour of her parting. Every morning, when she got up, she meant to say good-bye, but somehow another night came and the farewells were still unspoken.

She reproached herself (as well she might), and was still thus cruelly torn between two minds, when one night a dream visited her—the first for two months and more.

She dreamed that she was back at the *Beast's* palace, and wandering by a lonely path in the gardens which ended in a tangle of brushwood overhanging a cave. As she drew nearer she heard a terrible groaning, and running in haste she found the *Beast* stretched there on the point of death. Still in her dream she was bending over him when the stately lady stepped forth from the bushes and addressed her in a tone of grave reproach :—

'I doubt, *Beauty*, if even now you have come in time. Cruel, cruel of you to delay! when your delay has brought him so near to death!'

Terrified by this dream *Beauty* awoke in her bed with a start. 'I have done wickedly!' she cried. 'Am I too late? Oh, indeed I hope not!' She turned the ring upon her finger and said aloud in a firm voice: '*I wish to go back to my palace and see my Beast again!*'

With that she at once fell asleep, and only woke up to hear the clock chiming, '*Beauty*, *Beauty*,' twelve times on the musical note she so well remembered. She was back, then, at the palace. Yes, and—oh, joy!—her faithful apes and parrots were gathered around the bed, wishing her good morning!

But none of them could tell her any news of the *Beast*. They were here to serve her, and all their thoughts ended with their duty. Their good master—the lord of this splendid palace—what was he to them? At any rate nothing was to be learnt from them, and *Beauty* was no sooner dressed than she broke away impatiently, wandering through the house and the gardens to fill up the time until evening should bring his accustomed visit. But it was hard work filling up the time. She went into the great hall and resolutely opened the windows one by one. The shows were there as before; but opera and comedy, fête and pageant, held no meaning for her: the players were listless, the music was null, the processions passed before her eyes but had lost their power to amuse.

Supper-time came at length; but when after supper the minutes passed and passed and still no *Beast* appeared, then indeed *Beauty* was frightened. For a long while she waited, listened, told herself this and that, and finally in a terror rushed down into the gardens to seek for him. The alleys were dark; the bushes daunted her with their black shadows; but still up and down ran poor *Beauty*, calling to the *Beast*, and calling in vain.

She was drenched with the dew, utterly lost and weary, when, after three hours, pausing for a moment's rest, she saw before her the same solitary path she had seen in her dream: and there in the moonlight she almost stumbled over the *Beast*.

He lay there, stretched at full length and asleep —or so she thought. So glad was she to have found him that she knelt and stroked his head, calling him by name over and over. But his flesh was cold beneath her hand, nor did he move or open his eyes.

'Ah, he is dead!' she cried, aghast.

But she put a hand over his heart, and to her inexpressible joy she felt that it was still beating. Hastily she ran to a fountain near by, and dipping water into her palms from its basin she ran and sprinkled it on his face, coaxing him with tender words as his eyes opened, and slowly—very slowly —he came to himself.

'Ah! what a fright you have given me!' she murmured. 'Dear *Beast*, I never knew how I loved you until I feared that you were dead—yes, dead, and through my fault! But I believe, if you had died, I should have died too.'

'*Beauty*,' said the *Beast* faintly, 'you are very good if indeed you can love such an ugly brute as I am. It is true that I was dying for you, and should have died if you had not come. I thought you had forsaken me. But are you sure?'

'Sure of what?' asked *Beauty*.

'That you love me?'

'Let us go back to supper,' said *Beauty*, raising his head.

'Yes, let us go back to supper,' agreed the *Beast*, lifting himself heavily on her arm. He still leaned on her, as they walked back to the palace together. But the supper—which they found laid for two—seemed to revive him, and in his old stupid way he asked her about the time she had spent at home, and if her father and brothers and sisters had been glad to see her.

Beauty, though weary enough after her search through the park and gardens, brisked herself up to tell of all that had happened to her in her absence. The *Beast* sat nodding his head and listening in his old dull way—which somehow seemed to her the most comfortable way in the world. At length he rose to go. But at the doorway he put the old blunt question.

'*Beauty*, will you marry me?'

'Yes, dear *Beast*,' said *Beauty*; and as she said it a blaze of light filled the room. A salvo of artillery sounded, a moment later, from the park.

Bang, bang! fireworks shot across the windows of the palace; sky rockets and Roman candles exploded and a magnificent set-piece wrote across the darkness in letters of fire—'LONG LIVE BEAUTY AND THE BEAST!'

Beauty turned to ask what all these rejoicings might mean; and, with that, she gave a cry. The *Beast* had vanished, and in his place stood the beloved *Prince* of her dreams! He smiled and stretched out his hands to her. Scarcely knowing what she did, she was stretching hers, to take them, when above the banging of fireworks in the avenues there sounded a rolling of wheels. It drew to the porch, and presently there entered the stately lady she had seen in her dreams. It was the very same; and, all astounded as she was, *Beauty* did reverence to her.

But the stately lady was as eager to do reverence to *Beauty*. 'Best and dearest,' said she, 'my son is going to love you always; as how should he not, seeing that by your courage you have rescued him from the enchantment under which he has lain so long, and have restored him to his natural form? But suffer also his mother, a Queen, to bless you!'

Beauty turned again to her lover and saw that

he, who had been a *Beast*, was indeed the *Prince* of her dreams and handsomer than the day. So they were married and lived happy ever after ; nay, so happy were they that all over the world folks told one another and set down in writing this wonderful history of *Beauty and the Beast*.

MORAL

Maidens, from this tale of Beauty
Learn, and in your memory .write—
Daily leads a Path of Duty
Through the Garden of Delight;
Where the loveliest roses wear
Daunting thorns, for you to dare.

ANOTHER

Many shy, unhappy creatures
From the covert watch your mirth :
'Foul are we,' they mourn ; 'our features
Blot the sun, deform the earth.'
Pity, love them, speak them fair :
Half their woe ye may repair.